"Do you mind if I ask your name?"

"I don't remember."

"Like you have amnesia?"

"I think so. I really don't know."

"Great. Just great." Riggs swung his hand toward her. "Are these your kids?"

"I'm not sure."

They headed back down the winding road, the narrow pass surrounded by giant boulders.

"Be truthful. What's going on?"

A scowl crossed her face. "I. Don't. Know. I'm not even certain these are my kids."

Small rocks and dirt showered the hood of his truck.

He glanced up as a vast shadow teetered above them. He slammed on his brakes, and a boulder crashed in front of his truck.

"Hang on." Turning around to look out the back window, he floored it, guiding the truck through the tight turns.

"They found us!" the woman hollered. "We've got to get out of here."

"Cover the kids." He barely got the words out as more rocks rained down on his truck, the back window shattering with the impact.

Had the gunmen started the avalanche?

Connie Queen has spent her life in Texas, where she met and married her high school sweetheart. Together they've raised eight children and are enjoying their grandchildren. Today, as an empty nester, Connie lives with her husband and her Great Dane, Nash, and is working on her next suspense novel.

Books by Connie Queen

Love Inspired Suspense

Justice Undercover
Texas Christmas Revenge
Canyon Survival

Visit the Author Profile page at LoveInspired.com.

CANYON
SURVIVAL

CONNIE QUEEN

LOVE INSPIRED SUSPENSE
INSPIRATIONAL ROMANCE

LOVE INSPIRED® SUSPENSE

INSPIRATIONAL ROMANCE

ISBN-13: 978-1-335-55496-3

Canyon Survival

Recycling programs for this product may not exist in your area.

But when Jesus saw it, he was much displeased, and said unto them, Suffer the little children to come unto me, and forbid them not: for of such is the kingdom of God.
—*Mark* 10:14

I'd like to dedicate this story to Bruce—my best friend, husband and biggest fan. No matter if it's 4:00 a.m. or late at night, you always give me quiet time to work and have read through countless horrible chapters and answered panicked calls when I didn't know where to go next.

Love you. You're the best!

A special thanks to Dianne and Lynn for inviting me to stay on their ranch in Palo Duro Canyon. The place is absolutely gorgeous, but most of all, thanks for answering questions and offering suggestions.

As always, thanks to my wonderful critique partners and my editor, Tina James.

ONE

Warm, humid air blew against her cheek, stirring her brain to consciousness. The sticky heat was suffocating, and her chest struggled to inhale a breath as something sharp and hard jabbed her side. She forced her eyes open with great effort. Pain radiated throughout her body, and her hand jerked to the top of her head to ease the sudden aching throb.

Darkness lay before her, so thick and heavy, like a wool blanket on her shoulders even as stars filled the sky above.

Where was she?

She attempted to push the cobwebs aside, but something held her thoughts captive. Something was wrong.

Movement to the right caught her attention. Dark shadows towered beside her, blocking out even the stars. She whispered, "Is someone there?"

Thud.

Her hands quivered. She considered getting to her feet but was afraid movement would draw unwanted attention. She didn't know how or why, but danger felt close.

A mewing cut through the silence.

Her heart raced, nearly exploding.

Grit covered her hands. Dirt. She was covered in dirt. Her hand grasped the object behind her. Finally, she realized it was a sharp rock that poked her in the side of the back, causing her pain. She was sitting on some kind of huge stone.

Something brushed against her arm, and she jumped to her feet. Pain shot through her.

A cry split the night.

What in the world? Not the cry of a wild animal, but a baby.

Her hands grappled at her canvas belt and came away with a small flashlight. She clicked the button and pointed. The light landed on a young girl of about four years old and a baby dressed in navy blue.

Her breath hitched as confusion wreaked havoc in her mind. "Don't move."

The girl whispered, "You told us to be quiet and that we shouldn't use the light."

Before she could wrap her mind around the comment, a light flickered down below and something whizzed past her ear, followed by the resounding of a gunshot. Surprise spurred her into action. She scooped up the baby, and her light swung around into a deep canyon. They were on the edge of a cliff.

A scream escaped her throat, and her boot bumped into something small and hard, sending it falling below.

Bam. Bam. More gunfire. This time the shots originated from even closer, but the sparks of light were a hundred yards apart. There were at least two gunmen.

She clicked off the flashlight. "Come on. We have to get away from here."

The girl grabbed the back of her shirt, and they headed to the right, along the ledge.

Her mind raced as her instincts kicked in. They had to get to safety, but she didn't even know where they were or which way to go. Her hiking boot searched the solid ground before she took a step, followed by another. One step at a time.

The girl clutched the back of her top even tighter. She must be scared to death. The baby didn't make a sound as they continued along the rocky ledge.

A glance into the dark abyss didn't show movement or more gunfire. Could the gunmen still see them? Why were they pursuing them, anyway? Her brain struggled with the bombardment of questions, as she simply didn't know what was going on.

The flashlight had been in her belt. Did she have a cell phone? A quick pat down of her pockets turned up two full gun clips, but no gun. She checked again, but still nothing. Surely she had a phone.

Her foot struck something solid, and she came to a stop, causing the girl to run into her back. A sheer rock rose in front of her. Her toe searched the surface but only found a foot or so of solid ground before nothing but air. The shelf ended. Taking a deep breath, she whispered, "We need to go back."

"Okay," the little girl said. "Don't let me fall."

Her heart went out to her as she patted her on the back. "What's your name?"

"Kinslee LeighAnn. I'm four." She held up four fingers. "Kay-Kay is my nitname. And that's Jonah."

"That's a beautiful name." The baby seemed to be about six months old, since he had good control of holding his head up and could halfway hang on, but she really couldn't tell in the dark. "All right, Kay-Kay. You're safe with me. Stand right here, and I'll go around you."

Securing the baby on her hip, she placed her other hand against the rock for balance. "Here I go." She leaned in toward the wall and threw her outer foot on the other side of Kay-Kay, sandwiching the girl between her legs. Just as she went to move the other leg, a gunshot went off. She cringed and then swung her other foot around. "Come on."

Moving faster, she continued to lead them across the outcropping, back to their original spot. She had no idea how they got here, but they couldn't remain. Again, feeling with her toe, she persisted to cross the cliff. No more shots were fired, but that didn't mean their enemy wasn't close.

A couple of minutes later, the ledge again ended. Oh no. *Please, God, help us get down from here.*

Unless they parachuted in, they must've climbed here. If there was a way in, there must also be a way out.

"Wait." Bracing herself, she bent her knee and swung her foot down. At first, there was nothing, but then it touched something solid. She tested it before stepping down. She made certain the rock wouldn't give way before assisting Kay-Kay.

After twenty minutes of slow progress, they came to a flat, open area. The canyon was still below them, but hopefully they could find a shelter to hide in until daylight. Where were the gunmen? She and the children could very well be walking straight to them. The animals must not sense danger, for they had resumed their nighttime calls. The earlier humidity had lessened, replaced with a cool breeze. Jonah had fallen asleep on her shoulder. Her arm was killing her, but she had no choice but to keep going.

"I'm tired," Kay-Kay said.

She stopped and rubbed a hand across the girl's head. "I'm sure you are. You are such a strong girl, Kay-Kay." White teeth glistened back in the moonlight from the girl's smile. "Do you know where we are?"

Kay-Kay nodded. "Outside."

Okay. Ask an obvious question, you get an obvious answer. "Can you keep walking? Just a little more?"

"Yeah."

They continued on, the terrain much easier now. In the distance, a cow bawled. A ranch must be near, and hope soared. The more time passed, the more something kept bothering her. Why couldn't she remember anything? What was she doing here, and why were they in the canyon?

Whom did these kids belong to?

More importantly, who was she? She couldn't even remember her own name—the realization surreal. If the danger hadn't been serious, it might've been funny.

Among the juniper trees, a small light emerged. She kept her eyes trained on it, hoping her imagination wasn't playing games. Mesmerized, her focus remained on what she hoped was a ranch while watching for dangers. As they drew closer, a silhouette of a cabin came into view about a half mile away. A dog barked somewhere.

Kay-Kay's footsteps slowed. "I'm tired."

Oh no, not now. They had to keep going. They couldn't remain in the open like this. "Would you like to ride on my back?"

Kay-Kay let out an exhausted cry. "Can't we stop?"

"I wish we could, but we're almost there." She bent down and gently laid the baby on the ground while she helped Kay-Kay onto her back. "There. Are you up there?"

"Yeah."

She scooped up Jonah and climbed to her feet. Her arms rebelled with exhaustion, but pure determination and fear wouldn't allow her to quit. They'd taken only than three steps when the shadow of a man moved among the brush fifty yards away.

With a sharp intake of breath, she tightened both arms around the kids and ran in the opposite direction of the guy. A masculine laugh sounded behind her, urging her on. Lugging two kids put her at a disadvantage, so she headed straight for the trees.

If she could just lose him before he caught up to her.

Suddenly, brightness shone in front of her, illuminating her way. He had a light!

There'd be no hiding now. Footsteps grew louder as he closed the distance.

She darted between two trees when a strong arm shot out and pulled her under a limb. A hand clamped over her mouth.

She swallowed down the scream. Even with the children, she knew how to do one thing. To fight. She kicked out a boot and swiped it along the ground, connecting with legs. The hand clamped tighter on her mouth.

"Ow. Hold still. I won't hurt you." The Southern drawl shouted Texan.

Yeah, right. She kicked out again and missed. This time he drew her closer, the kids pressed between them.

A medium-size dog appeared at her leg and whimpered.

"Quiet, Shotgun." Then the man's warm breath brushed against her ear. "I'm not one of them."

Her mind raced, not believing him.

"I'm going to remove my hand. Don't make a sound."

She wanted to fight, but maybe she should wait until the gunman had passed. How could she attack three men while protecting the children? As if he read her thoughts, the man removed his hand and then quietly took Kay-Kay from her back. To her surprise, the girl didn't protest. Painful cramps plagued her biceps as she moved the baby to the other hip.

Now, maybe she could defend herself.

Riggs Brenner held the little girl against his chest as he watched the light bounce off the trees. The smell of baby shampoo wafted to him. His chest constricted as memories of his daughter flooded him. The pain—the emptiness—like it was yesterday. He hadn't held a child since that day, but this woman had left him with little choice. Well, he'd see to their safety as quickly as possible and leave them in the hands of the authorities.

Footsteps approached, and labored breathing filled the silence. The lady's pursuer hacked—a smoker's cough. By the sounds of his approach, he wasn't even trying to be quiet. No doubt the guy wasn't worried she would overtake him.

Riggs had seen another man earlier but didn't know his location now.

The gunman was careless and turned his back to them. Riggs took the lady's hand and whispered, "Stay low and follow me."

The woman slid her hand from his grasp but remained close as he wound his way through the brush. He had no idea what kind of trouble the lady had gotten herself into, but involving her two small children was just plain irresponsible.

They dashed through the thicket with Shotgun at the lady's side. The Australian shepherd had been trained to work cattle, but more importantly, he was a natural protector and had an uncanny ability to read Riggs's thoughts before he made them known.

Behind him, the baby whimpered. He turned. "Keep moving. We're almost to my place."

The woman didn't comment, but the way she traveled made him wonder if she had hiked in these conditions before. He had plenty of guns and ammunition at the house if need be. More importantly, his truck could take them into town, to the sheriff's office. It was a good hour's drive with getting through the canyon and then to town.

A beam of light shone on the juniper in front of him, and he stopped and waited. His house was only sixty yards away.

The baby cried again, this time louder.

More movement through the brush, and the light landed on the woman.

He set the girl on the ground and removed his Glock from his shoulder holster. "Take the kids and run." He pointed. "My house is through those trees."

He turned to Shotgun. "Assist."

The woman didn't reply but scooped up the girl and bolted for his house with both kids and his dog.

Riggs moved to the side of the tree, pointed his gun and said, "Stop. The lady is not alone."

But the man kept coming, his flashlight swinging wide toward Riggs, and then gunfire echoed through the canyon.

Riggs immediately returned two shots at the target. The gunman's flashlight fell to the ground, followed by a thrashing sound. "Don't come any closer. I'm armed." Riggs figured the man had already reached that conclusion, but it didn't hurt to reiterate the obvious.

Not knowing what he would walk into, Riggs decided to go after the woman and not approach the downed man. Keeping low, he jogged toward his house, staying as close to the trees as possible.

He stopped on the porch with his hand on the knob. "It's me. Riggs." He didn't want to startle her. "I'm coming in."

He let a second pass to allow the announcement to sink in, and then stepped through the door. A bark came from the back of the house toward his bedroom.

"Don't move."

He turned to see the woman holding his shotgun pointed at him. The two children were on the couch behind her. Anger at the ridiculousness hit him. "Put my gun down and get to explaining." He pointed his handgun at the door he'd just entered. "I don't have time for this. Those men might be right outside."

She didn't blink. "Who are you?"

His jaws clenched. She must be scared, but still… "Riggs Brenner. This is my ranch you're trespassing on."

"Why were you out there in the middle of the night?"

"Because someone was having a heyday shooting off guns." His eyes connected with hers. "Your kids don't need to be a party to this. Get in my truck, and

I'll take you to the sheriff's department. But lady, I don't take kindly to anyone, female or not, pulling my own gun on me."

The baby straightened his legs, pushed back into the cushions and let out a wail. The little girl wrestled to pick him up. Shotgun ran up and sat in front of them, his attention on the squalling boy. He nudged the baby with his nose.

"Oh, the doggie is so cute." The girl's face broke into a grin as she patted Shotgun's head. Even the baby stopped crying, his expression turning serious at the sight of the dog.

Riggs tried to keep his attention away from the children. The girl's curly blond hair was identical to Macy Sue's. A knife to the heart at the children's sweetness and innocence reminded him how important it was to protect them.

Shotgun wagged his tail and kept his focus on the young duo.

With one last glare at the lady, Riggs flipped off the lights and glanced out of the window. Surely the woman wouldn't shoot him, but he wasn't positive. "Do you have anything for the baby to eat?"

"I don't think so," she said.

That was an odd answer. The yard still appeared empty, and he detected no movement. "Let's go."

The woman clicked on her flashlight, keeping it pointed at the floor, and propped his gun in the corner. She took the baby from the child and glanced to Riggs. "Do you have anything for him to eat? I'm certain he's exhausted from being up all night and probably hungry."

Riggs couldn't exactly remember what babies ate at that age, but he grabbed a package of saltine crackers from the pantry and started to snag the gallon of milk from the refrigerator. Wait. A baby his age shouldn't have whole milk. He grabbed a can of apple juice from the shelf, opened it using a knife and set it on the counter with a plastic cup. The woman didn't carry a bag of any kind. "I don't have a bottle, and you need to dilute the juice."

"I think you're right. This will have to do." She poured the cup half-full.

While the lady prepped the food, he hurried back to his closet and nabbed more ammunition.

"Let's be quick." Grabbing his keys from the kitchen table, he headed out the back door. "Come, Shotgun." A swift survey didn't show anyone lurking outside. Keeping his Glock ready, he headed around to the driver's side of his 4x4 truck. Shotgun jumped in. "Back seat." The Australian shepherd leaped across the console and got into his place.

The lady climbed in on the passenger's side and settled both kids in her lap.

He put the truck into gear and took off. They whipped past his yard and onto the long driveway. The woman fumbled to give the baby a drink from the cup while the little girl huddled next to her. The bouncing from the sandy road caused the juice to splash.

"Sorry." He sighed. "Why are those men trying to kill you?"

"I have no idea."

Riggs glanced her way again. Unlikely she didn't know why they were after her. He took in her wavy red hair that was pulled back in a beige baseball cap, a cute but practical style if you're running around the canyon at night being chased by men with guns. Taking in her averted green eyes, he got the feeling he'd seen her before, which was silly. He'd lived on the ranch for nearly four years and had little contact with anyone. A lady that pretty wouldn't be easy to forget. Before moving here, he'd been with the FBI out of the Dallas office. He'd seen plenty of families' fights over kids turn deadly. "Was one of those men the father?"

Her head jerked toward him at the question. "I don't think so."

Why would she not answer honestly? She needed help. She had no vehicle or supplies for the children, and she was being pursued by at least two men.

The path eased right and around a boulder, the edge of the road a sheer drop-off to the canyon below. They steadily climbed higher.

"Listen, lady. I'm going to take you to the sheriff's department. I don't care what you tell them, but just a little friendly advice—it won't go well if you refuse to answer their questions." Couldn't she see how dangerous this was for the children? Why did people not cherish what they had? Guilt slammed him.

He'd failed his own wife and little Macy Sue.

The woman concentrated on giving the baby another drink and ignored him.

"How did you get into the canyon? Where's your vehicle?"

She inhaled a deep, exasperated breath. "I don't know."

He shoved his sleeves up his arms, suddenly hot. Fine. He'd tried.

His ranch was set miles from the main road and even farther from the closest town. People didn't accidentally come upon his place.

A little voice said, "Don't be mad."

Riggs glanced down at the adorable face, and his heart constricted. He forced a smile. "I'm not mad."

"My name is Kinslee LeighAnn, Kay-Kay for short. I'm four. That's Jonah, my baby brudder."

"Glad to meet you, Kay-Kay, who is four. My name is Riggs."

"I like your dog." Kay-Kay looked toward the back seat. "I used to have a dog. His name was Scout, but he was old and had to take a long trip."

"Oh." What could he say? Now he felt like a jerk for upsetting the girl.

"What's your dog's name?"

"Shotgun."

She giggled. "That's a funny name."

They neared the top of the peak, the pink of morning finally glowing in the east.

The woman said, "I appreciate your help, Mr. Brenner."

Those were the first normal words from the lady. Concern laced her voice, and he wished she would've let him know what was going on. Of course, with her having the children, it was better he didn't get more involved. He was no longer an FBI agent and didn't want to care for this family. Again, her features looked vaguely familiar. He'd tracked a lot of criminals during his career. Surely that's not where he'd seen her before. "Do you mind if I ask your name?"

Those green eyes looked straight at him. "I don't remember."

Yeah, right. A chuckle rose within him, but he swallowed it back. She continued to stare, the seriousness making him doubt she'd made it up. "Like you have amnesia?"

"I think so. I really don't know. I'm not trying to avoid your questions, mister. I simply have no answers."

"Great. Just great." He swung his hand toward her. "Are these your kids?"

"I'm not sure."

They headed back down the winding road, the narrow pass surrounded by giant boulders. There was less than a three-inch clearance on either side of his truck.

Anger boiled near the surface. Something wasn't right. Amnesia? No way. Her husband had probably won custody and she had gone to extremes to get her kids back. She didn't want to give her name for fear that Riggs would call it in. Not that he blamed her—he would've done the anything to have Macy Sue back. People needed to go through courts, though, and not drag their kids through dangerous canyons.

He hit the brakes as the steep decline made them gain speed. "Be truthful. What's going on?"

A scowl crossed her face. "I. Don't. Know. I'm not even certain these are my kids. I don't know where they came from. They don't *feel* like my kids."

His right eyebrow rose. "Seriously?" The callousness of the woman's words was unbelievable.

Small rocks and dirt showered the hood of his truck.

He glanced up as a vast shadow teetered above them. He slammed on his brakes and threw the truck into Reverse. His tires spun as he hit the gas, and a boulder crashed in front of his truck. The back bumper slammed into the side of the cliff, and children's screams filled the cab.

"Hang on." Turning around to look out the back window, he floored it, guiding the truck through the tight turns.

"They found us!" the woman hollered. "We've got to get out of here."

"Cover the kids." He barely got the words out as more rocks rained down on his truck, the back window shattering with the impact.

Had the gunmen started the avalanche?

Whatever the lady had done to make herself a target, these guys were playing for keeps and intended to take them all out. It'd been years since Riggs had been in law enforcement, but if he wanted to keep them alive, his protective instincts better kick in. And quick.

TWO

She tugged Kay-Kay close and leaned over the children. Thunderous booms sounded as rocks pelted the truck. Dust filled the cab, choking her.

The kids cried and coughed. Shotgun barked.

Riggs continued backing down the road much too fast, when suddenly the back end of the passenger side of the truck went off the road and dipped precariously over the side. Her breath caught, and she squeezed her eyes shut. *Please save us*.

The prayer had come out naturally, without thought. How could she not remember her own name but knew to pray?

The truck revved as the tires spun in the loose sand.

"Hold tight."

Every muscle in her body tensed as she tried to cover the children. Their screams only intensified the situation.

Switching back into Drive, Riggs floored it, but the vehicle barely moved, the roar of the engine deafening. Back to Reverse, he tried to rock the truck out. Finally, on the fourth try, the tire found traction, and the 4x4 shot backward, over a large rock, and continued the descent down the steep canyon.

She thought they'd made it when a new shower of debris rained on them. An enormous boulder tumbled down the side of the cliff, Riggs slammed on the brakes, but it was too late. The massive rock hit the bed of his truck, the vehicle jarring up and down.

Kay-Kay clamped her hands over her ears and yelled, "I don't like this! I want out!"

She wrapped her arms around the girl. "You're okay. I've got you."

Jonah's eyes were wide with fright, and his lip puckered as he watched his sister.

As more rocks slid, Riggs slammed the gearshift back into Park. "Get out. Get out. We have to make it down the cliff on foot."

His door was smashed against the rock wall, so he waited for them to get out of his way. With Jonah clinging to her shirt, she held on to him and opened the door. A ten-foot drop lay below them. If it were just her, she'd jump, but couldn't take a chance with the children. "Too steep."

Riggs climbed across the console into the back seat and opened the door. For a big man, he made it look easy. Shotgun stutter-stepped, gathering his courage before leaping out the door. Riggs followed suit. When his feet touched the ground, he held up his hands. "Let me have Kay-Kay first."

The four-year-old clung to her. "No! No! Don't drop me!"

"Riggs will catch you. Trust me." Her heart went out to the child, but there simply was no time. Prying Kay-Kay's hands away from her T-shirt, she dropped the girl into Riggs's waiting arms. Once Kay-Kay was safe, he held up his hands again. "The boy."

Grabbing the back of Jonah's onesie, she let him down as far as she could and then let go. He landed safely in the cowboy's grasp.

A rumbling told her another boulder was coming. She didn't have to think but vaulted from the vehicle, and her feet hit the unlevel ground beside Riggs. Her knees buckled, and she fell in the dirt just as a colossal stone crashed inches from her before continuing to descend the hill. More debris peppered the area.

"Get off the ridge. Come on." Riggs tugged on her arm, lifting her to her feet.

There was no time to think. She simply took Jonah as Riggs scooped up Kay-Kay, and they sprinted down the hillside just ahead of the avalanche. Her head pounded, as the earlier headache still hadn't subsided. The sharp incline increased her speed, and she leaned back to keep from falling.

A gigantic slab of rock rose up in front of them, half of it buried, the other end pointing heavenward. Riggs moved in front of her. "This way. Get behind the rock."

She did as he instructed, and they all huddled behind the slab as more rocks raced by. Jonah still cried, but the sound was drowned out by the slide, and Kay-Kay clung to Riggs for dear life. Shotgun barked and then joined them under the cover.

Moments later, silence replaced the deafening sounds. A glance to the truck showed it was entombed among the stones.

Riggs stared up, his gaze bouncing between the vehicle and the ledge above it. "That was no accident."

"I agree. At least I don't see anyone on the ridge."

"My truck is history." He merely glanced at her and turned down the slope. "We need to get out of here. Stick to the trees. We don't want to be caught in the open."

She hurried to catch up. "How far is the closest town?"

"At least twenty miles. There's no quick way through the canyon." Irritation clipped his voice.

"Point me in the right direction. I can get there on my own." She didn't know how or why, but she felt she'd been in tight situations before.

He stopped and glared. "No way. Who are you?"

"I told you. I don't know."

"Then I will call you Jane, as in Jane Doe."

She shrugged. "Fine by me." She didn't know why he was getting so upset. It's not like she enjoyed not being able to recall her life.

Kay-Kay tugged on Riggs's shirt.

"Hold on, darling. Give Riggs a minute." He started walking again with long, purposeful strides. "We need to know who is after you."

"Do you have a phone?" she asked.

"I do. It's in my truck." He shook his head. "Not that it matters—there's no reception here. I have an extra phone and a cell phone signal amplifier at the house, but it's spotty at best. I'll try it once we get back to the ranch."

"We can't go back. Those men will be watching for that."

He cocked his head at her. "Do you have any other suggestions, Jane?"

"Yeah. We keep going." The only thing that had kept her alive this long was to keep moving. But how did she know that? What part did she play with these kids? "You don't have any close neighbors?"

"Not this time of year. Except for the Poco Paya Ranch, which is twenty miles to the east, the neighboring ranches are deer leases. Occasionally, someone will camp for a few nights, but other than that, it's just me."

She looked again at the cowboy. She understood some people liked to get away and enjoy the country, but he was taking it to the extreme. Was he on the run from the law? He didn't look like the criminal type, but you could never tell. Maybe ranching was just a cover-up for his real purpose. Drugs?

Her instinct told her he was on the up and up, but she couldn't help but feel something was off. "Where exactly are we?"

"Palo Duro Canyon."

Palo Duro Canyon. She didn't think she'd ever been here before. It was somewhere near Amarillo. Where was home? She thought about it, and Texas had the right feel. But West Texas? She wasn't certain.

The pink of morning shone in the east, but the sun still hadn't topped the rise.

"I said I don't think we should go back to your ranch." She clasped her hands tight, trying to rein down the frustration. "It's not safe."

"Jane, what do you want from me?"

Kay-Kay tugged on his shirt again.

"What, darling?"

"That's Tormy. Her not Jane."

His gaze met hers before kneeling beside the girl. "Her name is Stormy?"

A smile crossed Kay-Kay's lips, and she nodded happily. "Yeah. Tormy."

"You're a smart one." Riggs tapped the end of her nose. "Do you know her last name?"

She wrinkled up her face and shrugged. "No."

Riggs stood and looked at her as he scrubbed the top of Kay-Kay's head. "Does Stormy feel familiar?"

No, not really. Maybe. "So-so." She rocked her hand back and forth. "Nothing feels right, so Stormy is as good as the next name."

Riggs didn't know what to think about the woman—Stormy. He picked up Kay-Kay and started walking again along the faint path, probably an animal trail, that would take him back to his house. "Contrary to what you want, we need supplies. There's no way we can travel twenty miles without more to drink and eat, mostly for baby Jonah."

"I get that, but don't you think we need to stay hidden?"

He forced a smile. "Yes. But it'll be near one hundred degrees in the canyon today. The kids won't survive."

"Then why don't you run back to the house and pack a bag, and we'll wait here for you."

What was she planning? He pressed his lips together. "And trust you not to make a run for it?"

"Do you have a choice?"

He would like to make it back to the house before it grew hot. He'd find his extra cell phone—a cheap flip phone he kept around in case something happened to his good one—and try to call Sheriff Rafe Ludlam to inform him of the situation. Riggs had only met the fifty-something lawman twice, but he'd listened to talk, and it appeared most believed Ludlam took his job seriously. A few people fussed, but he figured they were the type that would complain no matter who was in office.

Maybe she was right, and he should leave Stormy and the kids here. He could make better time and let them rest while he collected everything. He'd need more ammunition just in case they ran into the gunmen again. His canteens were in the barn. But most of all, he hoped to get that call in to the sheriff.

Suddenly, a memory surfaced.

What was he thinking? He couldn't leave them alone. Four years ago, he'd been working every night for two weeks and was supposed to have that Friday night off to celebrate his sixth wedding anniversary. But he'd chosen to work instead, hoping to bring the case to a close. His house blew up that night. Claire had been in the rocking chair reading Macy Sue her favorite book. If he'd taken his family out like he should have, he could've detected the danger and they'd still be here.

"We're all going together," he said. "Separating is out of the question."

Her eyes drew in, but she didn't comment, making it more awkward than if she'd argued.

Riggs knew nothing about Stormy, but he wondered if she'd earned the name.

As the day grew brighter, he kept an eye out for movement. Once he saw a deer high on the ridge, and a couple of times rabbits darted out from the underbrush. But nothing seemed out of place. Shotgun eagerly jogged along, spending most of his time in between Riggs and Stormy.

Where were those men, and what were they driving? He hadn't heard an engine. The canyon provided a natural barrier to most entrances to his ranch. The one road on which his truck was now buried was the only easy way in and out. There were a couple of other places, but a person would have to know where to look.

Stormy drew up beside him and fell in stride.

Kay-Kay was a tiny thing, but even so, the extra weight made walking difficult. Although Stormy hadn't complained, little Jonah must be tiring to carry. He had to admit, Stormy was a tough one. What was she doing in the canyon? No one accidentally came here. Amarillo sat sixty miles to the northwest. Over to the west thirty miles was Palo Duro State Park—a scenic place to bring the family and the RV for horseback riding, camping, bike trails and even a theatrical play. There wasn't much to the south and the east, except a scattering of farms and ranches.

Out of the corner of his eye, he noticed Stormy taking in their surroundings as well, no doubt watching for the gunmen. From the hiking boots to the khaki shorts with pockets to the cap to shield the sun from her eyes, the woman looked prepared for this type of activity. Coincidence or planned?

The feeling he'd seen her, or her picture, still gripped him. From where? He had worked a variety of cases with the FBI during his first years of being an agent. Mainly drug cases and, the last eighteen months of his career, human trafficking. The FBI had worked with other law enforcement in a coordinated effort to bring down the criminals at the top.

Could she be a suspect in one of his old cases? He'd noticed Kay-Kay hadn't called her Mama. Even Stormy admitted they didn't feel like her kids. Where had Stormy gotten Kay-Kay and Jonah?

The question weighed on his mind as they passed

Legends Cliff—a towering shelf of rock above the valley below.

"I need a break."

The abruptness of her words stopped him. "Okay. We should all take a moment. Kay-Kay, do you want to go with Stormy? I'll wait with Jonah."

The little girl nodded.

Stormy glanced at the girl, her lips pressed tight. No more than she'd made the gesture, the woman smiled. "Come on." She handed the baby to him and called over her shoulder, "We'll be right back."

Riggs positioned Jonah in the crook of his arm and stared after her. He had caught the disappointment in her expression at his suggestion of taking Kay-Kay. Why be hesitant in taking the girl along? Surely she wasn't considering running. "What is Miss Stormy up to?"

He glanced at Jonah and caught the boy's large brown eyes staring back at him. With a pang in his heart, he pulled the little fellow closer, savoring his warmth against his shoulder. Little fingers swatted at Riggs's face and then latched on to his bottom lip. The baby squealed with delight.

Riggs couldn't help but laugh as he closed his eyes against the assault. The boy's intense gaze continued, but Riggs couldn't afford to get distracted. Not only did he need to keep a lookout for the gunmen, but he also needed keep an eye on his pretty companion as well to make certain she didn't run off.

THREE

Stormy made her way through the brush and out of sight of the cowboy with Kay-Kay's hand in her own. A glance to the ledge on the cliff behind them reconfirmed her original belief. That was their position last night.

"Slow down." Kay-Kay's voice came out as a whine.

Afraid of being gone too long and causing Riggs to become suspicious, she scooped Kay-Kay into her arms. "Let's hurry."

The girl didn't say a word but looked around as they wove their way through the underbrush. A couple of minutes later, Stormy stood at the bottom of the cliff and searched the ground. She remembered kicking something off that ledge. Because of the clip in her pocket, she assumed the item to be a gun. With them being pursued, it couldn't hurt to have extra protection.

But what if it was something else? Something that proved her identity. If that were the case, she'd rather learn the information without Riggs's eyes seeing.

Large and small juniper trees littered the basin along with clumps of grass and flowering cactus. Small, shiny pebbles reflected in the sunlight, causing Stormy to do a double take to make certain it wasn't the gun. The scenery might've been beautiful if it wasn't for the danger of their situation.

"I need to go potty."

Stormy set the girl on the ground. "Go ahead. I'll make certain no one comes this way."

Kay-Kay frowned but moved to do her business.

Stormy's foot bounced up and down from nerves. It wouldn't take long for Riggs to come searching. Maybe the gun hadn't made it to the ground but got snagged somewhere on the way down. Her gaze browsed the cliff side, hoping to find her weapon, but the area was simply too vast.

"Okay." Kay-kay's denim shorts twisted at the waist, and Stormy helped her straighten them.

"Are you ready?"

The girl nodded, and when Stormy went around the other side of a mesquite bush, a glimmer caught in her eye. She blinked. Another glance and she saw a handgun lay in the sand just under a yucca plant.

Yes.

"Hold on. I have to grab something." Stormy hurried over to the weapon and picked it up. A Sig Sauer P365 Nitron semiautomatic pistol. She glanced at it no longer than a second before tucking it into the large pocket of her khaki shorts and secured the strip of Velcro to keep the pocket closed.

"Let's hurry." She spun around, ready to race back, but came to a stuttering halt.

"Find something interesting?" Riggs's pleasant tone didn't match the stone-hard glare. His boots were planted wide, and his chest moved up with a deep intake of breath.

She smiled, trying to disarm him. By his unblinking response, she'd guess the friendly gesture didn't work. She was tempted to avoid the question but decided against it. Riggs didn't seem like the type to be put off. Besides, what difference did it make?

"I found my gun." She patted her pocket. "I recognized the ledge we were on last night, and I remember hearing something fall. Considering I found an ammunition clip in my pocket, I figured it might be a gun. I was right."

His eyebrows knitted. "Anything else?"

"Not that I know of. I woke up on the ledge, was shot at and ran with the kids."

"What about this?" He held up a green backpack.

Her mouth dropped open. "Where did you find that?"

"A few yards back, over in a hollow. You recognize it?"

"No. But I wondered if I had dropped more while running." Her gaze connected with his brown eyes, and she tried to discern if he knew something. It was no use. She couldn't read Riggs. "Have you looked inside?"

He shook his head. "Not my place. It doesn't belong to me."

A mixture of relief and excitement flooded her as she took the bag from his outstretched hand. Maybe there'd be something inside telling her what she was doing here. She hurried to open the backpack and purposely turned her back a little so Riggs couldn't see over her shoulder.

Two unopened water bottles were in the outside pockets, one of them split open and void of liquid. Inside the main area were five or six diapers, a travel-size container of wipes, a new baby bottle with a square piece of cardboard still tucked inside with consumer information, a single-serving formula package, a pacifier, a size-5T pink shirt and shorts set, and a one-piece boy's outfit.

She knelt and carefully set the items on the ground so she missed nothing.

Jonah bawled and kicked his feet in a fit.

"Aw. He's probably hungry," she said. "I'll make him a bottle real quick."

Shotgun trotted over and sat, his tail thumping against the ground. Stormy kept an eye on the dog and baby, for she didn't how the two would take to one another. Jonah grew silent and intently watched the Australian shepherd. Riggs knelt beside his canine buddy so the boy could get close. Big, doggy sapphire eyes stared at the baby.

Jonah squealed, and his body shook with excitement.

Stormy laughed. "I think Shotgun's found a friend."

As she finished making the bottle, Kay-Kay also squatted beside the dog and cooed at him.

Riggs waited while she mixed the water with the powered formula. He held out his hand. "I can feed him while you finish going through the bag."

"Thanks." She glanced over at Riggs and smiled. Jonah was cradled in his arm and eagerly grabbed the bottle. "Looks like you have experience with kids."

His facial expression turned downward, and he avoided eye contact without replying. Okay. Fine. He was probably waiting to see if she found anything. Returning her attention to the bag, she checked the zippered pocket on the inside. Her fingers touched something with a smooth surface, and she removed a smartphone with the glass shattered. "I found a cell phone."

Riggs continued feeding Jonah but glanced up momentarily.

Please, please work. She hit the button, but no power. Was probably out of charge, or it could've suffered too much damage when she dropped the pack. She continued to search, hoping to find a wallet with a driver's license, credit card or identification, but there was nothing. Another tiny pocket was in the flip lid, one that most people never use. She unzipped it anyway and slid her hand in.

A business card. She read the words.

BTCHP
Bliss 903-555-2356.
3355 Maples Lane, Amarillo

The address had been handwritten in ink. A ripped-heart logo with the silhouette of a family covered the background.

She had no idea what the initials stood for and held it out to Riggs. "Does BTCHP mean anything to you?"

His eyes squinted. "No. And the area code isn't from around here, but somewhere in North Texas."

North Texas. Like maybe the Dallas area? Could be. "Do you think Bliss is a person or a town?"

"If it's a town, I've never heard of it. We can look up that Amarillo address when we get reception."

She stuffed the card back in her bag. "I'm afraid that's it."

"No identification?"

"Nothing. And I was really hoping I'd find something that told me what I was doing here. Like it'd contain a clue to who those men were that fired at me."

Riggs started walking again, and Stormy followed. Kay-Kay skipped along while often running her hand across Shotgun's fur.

Riggs said, "You didn't get here on foot, Stormy. Not with two kids. You were either in your own vehicle or were riding with the men."

That was a scary thought. Two men who wanted her dead.

Why? Were they after the kids or her?

Suddenly, the recollection of looking out of a dirty van window came to mind. It was dark outside, and a large block building sat on the other side of the street. A security light illuminated a crumbling parking lot. Overgrown shrubs lined the front glass doors and cast shadows into the alley between the building and a large trash dumpster.

The panicked cry of a child rent the night, sending chills down Stormy's spine.

"Let my sister go. Stop," a preteen girl yelled. "Don't touch me. Help! Someone, please help!"

Stormy looked on in horror as the older girl screamed and fought, but her attacker was too strong. The man in the shadows quickly moved toward the van, a bawling young child in his grip, and roughly dragged the older girl across the parking lot by her long hair. The girl fell, but he yanked her to feet. A light came on in one of the windows of the building.

A lump formed in Stormy's throat as she watched helplessly. *Please, God, someone help that girl.*

But it was too late. The man threw open the van door and shoved the kids into the cargo area.

Stormy's chest constricted at the memory, and she fought to catch her breath.

"Are you all right? What's wrong?"

The voice took a moment to penetrate her consciousness, and finally she glanced up to see Riggs watching her. "What?"

"What just happened? You're white as a sheet."

She swallowed, uncertain what to say. Had the vision been a memory? Something she had witnessed? Or something sinister she had taken part in? "Nothing. I'm fine."

He stared at her. No doubt she wasn't fooling him, but she simply couldn't talk. Dryness pricked at her throat, and her T-shirt suddenly felt sticky and suffocating.

Someone help that girl. The words uttered in the quick prayer replayed through her thoughts. Had someone come to the children's aid?

She glanced from Kay-Kay to Jonah. Her chest tightened at the thought of the men firing bullets at them. What if she had remained unconscious on that ledge? What if one of the children had fallen to their death and or been hit by a bullet? Riggs was right. They couldn't stay in the open like this. They'd have to take the chance no one was watching the ranch. "Let's get these kids to safety now!"

Concern for Stormy ate at Riggs. Something had just happened. He didn't know what it was, but he knew she was keeping it from him. Had her memory returned? What did she recall? By her expression, it couldn't have been good.

For the next twenty minutes, they walked along in silence, the events replaying through his mind. After Jonah finished his bottle, the boy fell asleep, and Riggs handed him to Stormy while he carried Kay-Kay, her head snuggled against his shoulder. It was much too far for the four-year-old to walk, and she hadn't muttered a word, making him wonder if she'd drifted off to sleep, too.

Finally, his cabin came into view. It played peekaboo among the trees, giving him a glimpse of the structures here and there. He'd kept an eye out, and now he took his leisure looking over his place. His herd was normally at the south end of the ranch at the noon hour, so it didn't surprise him that his cattle weren't in sight.

There weren't any vehicles or movement outside his home. As good as any watchdog, horses were excellent at giving a warning of something amiss. Jack and Honey munched grass in the corral outside the barn and didn't look up until Shotgun ran out from the brush. That was a good sign.

"When we get to the house, I'd like for you and the kids to wait in the barn while I check out the cabin. Keep Shotgun with you."

"Okay. Do you have another vehicle?"

"Not that runs. The transmission in my old truck finally gave out, and I haven't had the time or the money to repair it."

Stormy repositioned Jonah higher on her arm and then dug her Sig out with the other hand. She removed the magazine from her pocket and briefly examined it before sliding it into the gun. She set the thumb safety and slid it into her pocket.

It was in him to ask if she knew how to use the weapon, but he refrained. Certainly, if she could load and unload the pistol, she'd been taught to use one.

As they approached the barn, he led the way around

the north side, out of sight from the house. He set Kay-Kay at Stormy's feet. "Wait here."

Stormy nodded.

Quickly, he went in and checked the hiding places to make certain no one was inside the barn. After a thorough search, it didn't appear anyone had been there. Anticipation at calling the sheriff swirled in his gut. Hopefully, he could contact the department and be back about his normal business within a couple of hours. He opened the side door and whispered, "Come on in. It's clear."

Stormy silently stepped through the door and glanced around at the stalls and square bales stacked neatly in the corner. What did she think of his place? There was plenty of grass for the summer, but Riggs already had a good supply of hay cut for the winter.

Few people had been on his ranch, for he'd built it three years ago and rarely had visitors. Once his brothers and mom visited. Another time, an old friend from the FBI brought his family out for a "roughing it" mini vacation in his upstairs loft, complete with air-conditioning and toilet facilities. Riggs smiled. He didn't blame them for not wanting to sleep on the ground with all the critters and snakes.

What would Claire have thought of the barn and house? They'd purchased the land when they'd first married, and he'd thought there were no structures on it. Later, he'd accidentally come upon a decrepit ranch house hidden near the rim of the canyon while searching for a lost calf. The location provided shelter from the sun and heat, but not much of a yard. But after his wife and daughter died, and he determined to build, Riggs decided on the current location for a home. The view was spectacular, and he didn't have to worry about flash floods.

Shotgun put his nose down and got busy smelling the inside of the stalls. A horse blanket lay atop a saddle, and Riggs moved it onto a pile of hay. "I brushed the blanket the last time I used it. It should be fine to lay Jonah on."

"Thanks." She laid the boy on his back. "My arm is killing me."

"I can imagine."

Kay-Kay plopped beside Jonah and laid her head on the blanket.

Riggs turned to Stormy. "I'll be right back. You've got your gun, just in case. I'll leave my dog with you."

"Take Shotgun. He may notice if something's not right before you do."

"Okay."

He turned to leave, but she grabbed the sleeve of his Western shirt. "Thank you. You didn't have to help us like this, and I really do appreciate it."

Her green eyes stared back at him. Once again, he thought he'd seen those intense eyes before. "You're welcome. Let me check everything out, and I'll be right back."

As he shut the barn door, a strange protectiveness enveloped him like he hadn't felt since Claire and Macy Sue. But Stormy differed from Claire in many ways. His wife had been content living in the suburbs with a small yard and no pets to tend to. She enjoyed her weekly date with two other moms from the neighborhood who also had young children. He could never imagine Claire hiking through the canyon with two kids. And if Riggs couldn't keep his gentle wife safe, what made him think he could protect a gun-wielding, confident woman who wasn't afraid to meet adversity head-on like Stormy?

Keeping an eye out, he moved swiftly toward his house and away from Stormy and the kids. He was ready to call the sheriff and turn them over to the authorities. Stormy knew nothing about him, didn't know he'd let his own family down.

"Heel," he commanded. Shotgun fell in behind him.

Birds flew from the trees as he crossed the yard to the carport and to the back door. There were no new tracks that he could determine. He'd left the house unlocked, and after glimpsing inside a window, he slowly opened the door.

Nothing stirred, and cool, air-conditioned air hit him. With his gun ready, he stepped inside. Normal humming from appliances and the clock ticking were the only discernible noises.

Careful to be quiet, he made his way through the house, looking for any sign of an intruder, with Shotgun right behind him. No muddy footprints and nothing out of place. When he got to his bedroom, he performed a quick check of his closet. Except for the shotgun Stormy had left in the living room, his weapons and ammunition were still there. He exhaled a breath and dropped his gun to his side.

Swiftly walking into the living room, he snatched his flip phone from the mantel, hoping his cell amplifier could get a signal. He riffled through the pantry and took some bottles of water and a box of breakfast bars and headed toward the back of the house.

Shotgun barked. The dog ran through the dining area and pawed at the exit.

Riggs hurried and then eased the door open. His

gaze took in the empty yard before noting the barn door stood wide-open. Shotgun barked again and sprinted across the lawn.

Kay-Kay screamed.

With his gun ready, Riggs ran to the side of the building and dropped his supplies to the ground. As much as he'd like to rush in, it might get Stormy or the kids killed. Adrenaline pumped through his veins, and he peered inside.

"I got her." A clean-cut thirtyish man held a pistol pointed directly at Stormy's chest. He called over his shoulder, "Leave the child alone. Go take down the cowboy in the house."

Stormy's Sig lay at her feet in the hay.

A heavy man with long, scraggly hair held Kay-Kay by the arms. A small rip in his jeans on the outer thigh, surrounded by a dark patch, suggested he was probably the man Riggs had shot last night. By the way he moved, the injury wasn't too severe.

Tears ran down Kay-Kay's face as she fought against his hold. "Let me go!"

Shotgun ran straight to the girl and went into a barking frenzy at the man.

"Get away, mutt." The man kicked out but didn't connect and then shook Kay-Kay. "Hold still, little brat, before I wallop you."

"Don't hurt her." The man with the gun didn't let his attention stray from Stormy. "We were told to bring them back safely. Hurry up and do as I say."

"You go take care of the cowboy, Waylon. I'd be glad to handle her."

"Shut up, stupid. No names," Waylon snapped.

"Why, they can't do anything. I'm Sonny. Sonny," the heavy man taunted.

Jonah cried and wiggled on the saddle blanket, no doubt awakened by the chaos.

Stormy stared directly at Waylon. If she was scared, she didn't show it.

Until Sonny released Kay-Kay, it'd be risky to make a move. And if Riggs shot Waylon, the weapon could go off and kill Stormy. Riggs drew a deep breath, raised his Glock and prepared to take action.

Please help me save them, Lord. It was his first prayer in years.

But even as he thought the words, Stormy took a step forward, and Riggs realized he was too late. She was taking the matter into her own hands.

FOUR

As Riggs looked on, Stormy momentarily met his gaze before she looked away, evidently not wanting to draw attention to him. She grabbed the barrel of the gun with her left hand and, in one swift move, hit Waylon's wrist with her right. She twisted the weapon toward him.

Shock registered on the gunman's face. He yelled and released his grip.

Stormy aimed the pistol at Sonny while he held Kay-Kay. "Drop your weapon."

Riggs stepped through the door and aimed his Glock at Waylon. The man clutched his fingers close to his body. No doubt, Stormy's move probably broke his trigger finger.

Jonah's cries turned into screams.

Shotgun growled and barked viciously at the man holding Kay-Kay. Sonny jerked back as he looked around, evidently not liking the odds. Suddenly, he shoved Kay-Kay toward Stormy and sprinted out the side door. At the same instant, Waylon ran past Riggs and out the door.

Riggs could've shot the man but held his fire. He didn't want to upset the children any more than they already were. He hurried over to Jonah and scooped him into his arms. His gaze cut to Stormy. "Are you all right?"

She held Kay-Kay in her arms and pulled her tight. "Yeah."

"I'll be right back." He handed Jonah off to Stormy. "I need to make certain those two are gone."

"Be careful."

He exited the main door with his gun ready. An engine revved somewhere. A dust cloud appeared, and a burgundy newer-model truck raced across the hill behind his home. Suddenly, the truck slowed, and an arm appeared out of the passenger window, something in the man's hand.

As Riggs's mind fought to unscramble what he was seeing, it dawned on him.

Boom!

Riggs flew backward, heat engulfing him, and slammed into the side of the barn. Pain radiated throughout him. Fire and debris rained from the sky as a black cloud lifted into the air.

His ears rang, and dizziness dropped him to his knees.

Shotgun sprinted past him and toward the hill.

Riggs yelled, "No! Come back!"

Stormy appeared at his side. Her hand touched his shoulder, and he flinched at the contact. Her mouth moved, but he couldn't hear anything.

The truck. Where were the gunmen? His gaze searched the hill, but there was no sign of their vehicle. As if she understood, Stormy held the pistol she'd taken from Waylon and looked around. Then she knelt beside Riggs.

"Are you injured?" Her voice was faint but there.

"I don't think so." He struggled to his feet. "The kids. Stay with the kids." He found his Glock on the ground, dusted it off and then proceeded to the side of the barn. He peeked around the corner. A dust cloud in the distance, a telltale sign that the truck fled up the trail that led to the back side of his ranch. Shotgun jogged toward him.

Stormy came up behind him, Jonah in her arms and Kay-Kay at her side. The baby still had tears in his eyes. She asked, "Is there anything I can do?"

He shook his head and instantly regretted it. "Wait, yeah. See if you can find my flip phone."

His house now lay in bits and pieces on the ground. Only the concrete slab remained. His heart constricted. Why were these guys after them? And Waylon had said they weren't supposed to hurt the children, but then they blew up the house.

Had they changed their mind?

As he stared at the debris, memory of FBI Agent Johnny Callahan entering the office with a police officer at his side squeezed Riggs's chest, threatening to take his breath away. The dread on the agent's pale face, along with avoiding eye contact, was indescribable. And then the officer's words—*Agent Brenner, there's been an explosion at your house. Your wife and daughter did not make it.*

At the time, Riggs knew it had to be a misunderstanding. He'd just spoken with Claire. She'd called to tell him she had canceled their dinner plans and let the babysitter know she wouldn't be needed. Claire planned to spend the evening with Macy Sue. He promised he'd make the date up the following night.

He'd rushed home, only to find there was no home. Just a pile of rubble and smoke still rising from the smoldering ashes. Even before the funeral, Riggs had believed the explosion was a criminal act—a vengeful deed of some angry person he had sent to prison. But after the fire marshal had repeatedly confirmed a gas leak under the house and no evidence of foul play, Riggs had gone on a downward spin, trying desperately to answer why.

If he'd only been with his family like he was supposed to, they wouldn't have been home when it exploded. Macy Sue would've been at the sitter's place, and Claire would've been at the new Italian restaurant with him.

For the next few months, Riggs had tried to bury himself in his caseload to deal with the loss and guilt, but he couldn't concentrate and made a couple of senseless mistakes. His lieutenant commanded he take two weeks off for bereavement, and Riggs went fishing at a friend's lake cabin. Instead of peace, he spun further into an emotional black hole, hating himself for the choices he'd made and craving a do-over. Since that was impossible, he finally saw the FBI therapist at the urging of friends and family. Months later, he quit the FBI and moved to his ranch in West Texas.

"Are you okay?"

His gaze went back to Stormy, her intense green eyes full of worry. "What did you say?"

"Are you okay? I'm sorry about your house." Stormy held out his black cell.

He took it as he looked directly into her green eyes, concern staring back at him. Her red hair was askew underneath the baseball cap. No, he didn't want to talk about his house. "Would you like to tell me what all that was about?"

"I don't know. I've already told you, I can't remember."

"You've had training. You executed a perfect maneuver in taking Waylon's gun and probably broke the man's finger."

She glanced away.

He had no idea whom or what he was dealing with here. But one thing was clear—the danger was much bigger than he'd imagined. The men had set off an explosive using a remote detonator. Street thugs or ex-boyfriends didn't have those just lying around.

He didn't know who or what Stormy was, but those men wanted her dead, and someone else was calling the shots. And that meant the gunmen would return, probably with more firepower.

No one had been more surprised than Stormy when she disarmed Waylon. The action had come instinctively, like it was a part of her. Deep down, she knew she could fight. Kay-Kay and Jonah weren't her children. She realized that, too. Maybe it wasn't so much what she could remember, but what she perceived—felt.

She finally responded, "You're right."

Riggs glanced at her. "Have any other memories returned?"

"Not really." Except for the one earlier where the girls were thrown into the van. Should she tell Riggs about that? Stormy didn't know what it meant. For all she knew, it could've been something she'd seen on television. But she didn't think so. It felt like she had witnessed an abduction. She stared at him. "I have a feeling, though, that I'm here on a mission."

"What kind of mission?"

She shrugged and pushed Kay-Kay's hair out of her face. "I assume it has something to do with these two."

Riggs seemed to consider this as his eyebrows turned inward. "For now, let's assume that's true. We need to get to safety, hopefully in the protection of the sheriff's department, so we can sort this out."

Shotgun returned and lay down at Riggs's feet, panting heavily.

She asked, "What about your cell phone?"

He opened it and punched in 911. After a couple of seconds, he snapped it shut. "Nothing. I was afraid of that."

"Is there anywhere you get reception with your booster around here?"

"It just blew up with the house." He turned and pointed at the top of a tall ridge. "Sometimes I can get reception several miles over there with my cell. Depending on the weather, sometimes closer."

She sighed and glanced heavenward. The afternoon was already unbearably hot. Why anyone would want to live this far outside town was beyond her. "Is there any way to get there other than walking?"

His jaw tightened. "I could leave you and the children in the barn, but I don't want to do that. Especially after this last attack."

"How many guns and ammo do we have?"

He shook his head. "No. I will not chance your safety."

"I have my Sig and Waylon's Smith and Wesson

Shield .45," she continued, like he hadn't spoken. "You have your Glock. Do we need more?"

"We're not separating."

Stormy put her hand on her hip and shook her head before turning and walking over to the pen. The two horses jogged from one end of the enclosure to the other.

"I wasn't referring to being left here. But what about your horses? Can we take them?"

Riggs followed. "I'd only trust Honey, the palomino. She's twelve and calm."

She walked straight to the Appaloosa. A large, big-boned gelding. "And what's wrong with him?"

"Nothing is wrong with Jack. But he's five and spirited."

As Stormy held her hand out, the gelding tossed his head and then galloped across the pen. No doubt the explosion had him spooked.

"Do you sense you can ride a horse?"

Did she detect a little sarcasm in Riggs's tone? She scrutinized him but couldn't tell. His short-sleeved blue plaid Western shirt contrasted with his eyes, bringing out gold flecks in the rich chestnut brown. No man should get by looking that good without a warning sign. "I'm willing to try to ride. And I don't intend to stand around talking about it."

Riggs let out a low sigh-growl, and she almost laughed at his response.

He said, "We can try it. You ride Honey." He glanced at the kids. "I'll take Kay-Kay with me."

She turned to the little girl. "Would you like to ride the horse?"

Kay-Kay beamed and clapped her hands together in excitement. "Yes."

Fifteen minutes later, Riggs had both horses saddled while she had filled the canteens and water bottles. She gathered the food Riggs had dropped on the ground and found Shotgun's dog food in the barn and put it all in her backpack. Having just changed Jonah and given Kay-Kay a breakfast bar, Stormy stepped into Honey's saddle, and Riggs handed her the baby.

The one family-size box of breakfast bars wasn't much, but hopefully they could call for help and pick up supplies when they got to a town.

"Kay-Kay bug, come stand on a feed tub," Riggs said.

The girl giggled, her eyes glistening with joy. "Bug? I'm not a bug."

"Whatever you say, Kay-Kay bug." A smile tugged at his lips as he settled on Jack. He rode over and picked the girl up, putting her in front of him. Stormy didn't think Kay-Kay's denim shorts looked long enough to provide protection for the girl's legs, but hopefully the ride wouldn't take long.

She watched to see how the horse would react to a child being on his back, but Jack didn't even seem to notice. Stormy didn't know if she'd ever ridden and was just a little nervous.

"How long will this take?" she asked.

"Two to three hours if we have no trouble." He looked at her. "Are you okay with that?"

"What choice do I have?"

"Touché." He led the way as Stormy nudged her heels into the palomino's sides. "Honey should follow with no problems."

Riggs headed past what used to be his house. He had said little about the loss. He had gone out of his way to help her, and she greatly appreciated that. Riggs was a good-looking man. Muscular build, Western clothes and, besides a five o'clock shadow, he was clean-cut. His dark tan shouted that he spent many hours outside. What was a man like him doing out here alone? She would've thought he had a wife and kids. She didn't know his age, but she'd guess in his thirties.

Who was she kidding? She didn't even know how old she was. Maybe thirty? Late twenties? It was weird not to know these things about herself. Did she have a family waiting for her? A husband? She glanced to her left hand, even though she had already noticed she wore no ring. What about her parents? Were they still alive?

If she had family, she hoped they weren't worried about her. How did a person even go about finding out who they were? In the movies and books, people with amnesia always recovered. She prayed that was the case with her.

Honey was tall, and her gait was smooth. Even though Stormy held the reins, the horse didn't pull against it. Riggs, on the other hand, had to keep a firm grip on Jack. The horse seemed eager to run.

Jonah drifted off to sleep again. Poor fellow. Sleeping in small chunks couldn't be very restful. His bottom rested against her legs, and he leaned back against her stomach, which relieved some of the pressure on her arm. She'd be sore tomorrow.

After a few more minutes, they topped out on a rise and Riggs pulled his phone out of his shirt pocket. He turned it on, pushed a few buttons and glanced to the screen.

"Anything?"

He shook his head. "No signal."

They continued in silence, each of them in their own thoughts. Kay-Kay didn't say anything but appeared content. Stormy couldn't wait to find out who was after them. How could you fight an unknown enemy?

The vision of the girls being kidnapped and then shoved into the van kept replaying through her mind. It seemed so clear and close. Like it was an important moment in her life. Where did this happen and when? Was it what led her to Kay-Kay and Jonah? Or were these kids kin to her, like a niece and nephew? So many questions and not enough answers.

"Are you thirsty?"

Riggs's voice pulled her out of her thoughts. "A little. I'd appreciate a drink."

He stopped and dug into his saddlebag. She kept the breakfast bars in her backpack while he carried the drinks.

As he handed her a bottle, his fingers brushed against hers. Electricity shot through her at his touch, and she jerked back. Quickly, she took a swig, hoping he didn't notice her strange reaction.

What was wrong with her? Surely she didn't normally act this way when around a male.

She took another swallow and then handed the bottle back. After Kay-Kay drank, they were again on their way. Should she ask her next question? It wasn't like they had anything to do while riding. "Why do you live way out here alone?"

He didn't even look at her. "I prefer it that way."

Evidently. "Have you always ranched?"

This time, he pulled on the reins and turned to her, his look serious. "No, I haven't. But it's what I want to do now."

His glare didn't scare her none. She thought it more defensive than offensive. "Were you raised around here? Went to school here?"

He cleared his throat. "I grew up on the southwest side of Amarillo and went to school there. My parents farmed cotton. I graduated from Texas Tech. Do I pass your test?"

Her eyes narrowed as she studied him. He was hiding something, that much she knew. And she supposed it was none of her business. She just felt like, well, she didn't know. Maybe that she'd feel better about not knowing who she was if she knew more about Riggs. But that was silly, of course.

"I don't mean any offense," she finally answered.

"Good. What I'm doing here has nothing to do with you." He nudged his horse.

Honey again fell in line behind them. The longer Stormy stared at Riggs's broad back and considered his defensiveness, the more she believed he was hiding something. But what? And why did she even care, except maybe because she felt indebted to him? She didn't know how she normally acted around men, but she found herself drawn to this cowboy. He was quiet, which suited her fine.

Which brought up another question. How come no one had come looking for her except for the gunmen? No family or coworkers. Did anyone know where she was? Did anyone care? Or was she a loner like Riggs? The thought made her cringe.

Maybe she'd neglected to share her plans, and several people were looking for her. Yes, that's what she chose to believe. Kind of like that movie where the guy was stranded on a deserted island for years, and when he returned home all his friends threw him a party.

The image of the kidnapped girls returned to her mind, along with the feeling she was on a mission. A mission for what she didn't know, but she figured she was just like Riggs. Alone with secrets that she could share with no one.

FIVE

Riggs could feel Stormy watching him as they rode up the canyon path. He didn't even know her, and he certainly hadn't invited her onto his ranch. His past was not up for discussion. He had barely spoken to Claire's parents since his wife died. They had reached out multiple times, but Riggs had purposely kept the interaction short. How could he look his in-laws in the face when they were a reminder of everything he'd lost?

Even though Claire's family had never voiced it, they had to believe their deaths were his fault. His wife had made it no secret that she wanted Riggs to be home more. If he'd been out celebrating their anniversary like they'd planned instead of staying at work, his wife and daughter would still be alive today.

A lump formed in his throat, making it difficult to swallow. Stormy didn't realize it yet, but she couldn't depend on him to protect them. Claire had accused him more than once of putting his needs first.

What was he supposed to do with this lady? It'd be smart to deliver them to the sheriff as soon as possible. It hadn't escaped his attention how attractive Stormy was, or how her curly red hair fell against her shoulder. Or how those intense green eyes seemed to sparkle with life.

His heart squeezed. And then there were the kids. Kay-Kay was just about the size of Macy Sue. The blond hair and blue eyes were identical. How was a man supposed to put that behind him? Would the pain ever go away? *Time heals all wounds* was a farce.

It'd been four years since their deaths, and he still thought of his family every night. He imagined what Claire would say about the ranch, about the colorful red Indian blankets or the purple tansy aster in full bloom, or the beauty of a spring lightning storm from the safety of the back porch. Occasionally, he'd see a toy in a store and think about how Macy Sue would enjoy playing with it. The only thing that had faded with time was him jumping for the phone when it rang in hopes it was his wife.

Claire was never coming home.

She'd never call to ask him to pick up something on the way home from work. Macy Sue wouldn't be calling to tell Daddy good-night when he was working late at the office.

He'd give everything he owned to hear their voices one more time.

A gust of wind kicked up the dust, and the clouds drowned out the sun. It was a respite from the afternoon heat.

If it weren't for Stormy and the kids, he would've gone almost straight up the canyon, but he thought it safer to wind up the path. There'd been no sign of the gunmen or the burgundy truck. He was under no delusions that someone who had tried that hard to harm them would give up now.

A rabbit darted out from under a bush and continued running in front of them.

Kay-Kay pointed. "Aw. A bunny."

Shotgun came to attention and danced in place, almost as if asking for permission to pursue the animal.

"Stay." Riggs knew his dog desired to chase. The rabbit hopped off to the right and disappeared. Shotgun waited with his ears perked and tail wagging, then trotted to catch up to them.

As the afternoon dwindled away, the clouds swirled, and the wind continued to blow. He shifted in the saddle and picked up the pace. They needed to be on solid ground and not on the side of the canyon if a storm blew in. Flash flooding wasn't out of the question.

Over the rim, a streak of lightning flashed and splintered.

"That looks like a bad one," Stormy commented. "Is there a good place to hole up?"

He glanced over his shoulder. "Not that I know of. But the hills are full of crevices and deep cuts. We'll find a place."

A powerful gust blew dirt into his face, and he leaned forward into the wind, trying to keep the dust out of his eyes. Kay-Kay whined and rubbed her hair out of her face. The juniper trees bent under the force. They needed to take the kids somewhere safe. The old home place had a building. Not nice, but it would provide shelter from the elements. It was another thirty minutes away.

A deep rumble ripped through the canyon, and big drops of rain pelted the ground.

He searched the area, but all he could see were rocks and scruffy trees. The home place was high up, near the rim. It was one of the few places where he knew he would receive reception. He just needed to get them out of the gorge and to the authorities. Looked like they'd have to wait the storm out first.

Up the canyon wall, less than a quarter of a mile away, a dark hole appeared among the rocks. That had to be a cave. Riggs pointed. "Right there. We're headed to that cave."

"Okay."

Lightning streaked, followed by *boom!*

Jonah let out a wail at the sudden noise.

Thunder shook the ground, and Jack threw up his head. Riggs kept a tight grip and glanced over his shoulder at Stormy and Honey. The palomino's ears were back, but at least she wasn't fighting the reins. Stormy held on tight to Jonah, who was wide-awake, his face wrinkled into a frown. The woman appeared calm.

Kay-Kay trembled.

"I've got you. It's just a storm." He pulled the girl a little closer. Jack threw his head up again and tried to turn back down into the canyon, but Riggs tugged on the reins and insisted the animal continue. The horse's spirit was something to be reckoned with, but he was sure-footed on these canyon trails. The few times Riggs had ridden in the rain, it had always been on Jack.

More lightning splintered across the sky.

Jack stepped sideways and again tried to turn back, but Riggs kept a firm grip. The skies opened up, and within seconds, rain soaked them through to the skin. His trench coat had blown up with the house, but he wished he had it now to wrap around the girl. One more glance at Stormy told him she was as determined as he. Her eyes squinted against the rain, but she kept coming.

As they arrived at the path leading to the cave, he turned in the saddle. "Let me check it out first!"

A bright light flashed just as thunder rumbled and the earth shook.

The girl cried. "I want my mama."

"You'll be okay, Kay-Kay bug." He gave her shoulder a gentle squeeze. "I've got you."

"Let me take her." Stormy motioned with her hand.

He didn't like having both children on one horse and started to say so, but then he glanced down at Kay-Kay. Her big, trusting blue eyes stared back. He swallowed. She'd probably be safer on Honey with the horse's calm disposition. Riggs rode up beside the palomino and swung Kay-Kay in front of Stormy.

Jack raised his head and whinnied, but Riggs kept the beast under control as they headed toward the cave opening. The animals would simmer down once they were in the shelter and out of the storm. The rocky trail led upward and then leveled out.

When they were about twenty feet from the entrance, Jack refused to comply, tossed his head and, stepping high, danced sideways. What was wrong with the horse? He didn't normally rebel. "Whoa, boy."

Stormy yelled. "Watch out!"

Jack's back hoof slid on the wet rock. The horse stumbled and almost went down. When he regained his footing, he reared up.

"Whoa. Whoa." Riggs had to get off this horse. He couldn't wait any longer. Throwing his leg over the saddle, he jumped off the animal and landed hard on the ground. Instead of fighting to control Jack, which could injure one or both of them, Riggs released the reins.

Jack took off at a gallop down the canyon.

Honey was wide-eyed and looked ready to bolt after the other horse. Riggs hurriedly took Kay-Kay and Jonah.

Stormy dismounted Honey but retained a hold on the reins and tugged them toward the opening. As they neared the cave entrance, Honey whinnied and leaned back.

"Come on, Honey," Stormy cooed. "We're almost there."

"Here. Take the kids. Give me the reins." After both kids were out of the way, Riggs took the leather straps and tried to lead her into the opening and out of the storm. But Honey drew back and fought with each step. What was the matter with the horses?

Finally, he persuaded Honey to enter the rock cavity, but the animal continued to tremble.

Stormy and the kids stood off to the side. She reached for the flashlight on her belt.

Lightning constantly flashed, but at least they were out of the downpour.

The shrill of an animal screaming came from the deep.

Chills marched down Riggs's spine. He faced Stormy. "Stay back!"

Shotgun barked but remained beside the kids. Stormy pointed the light. The eyes of a cougar glowed in the reflection. A display of long, white fangs had Riggs taking a step back. The enormous cat hissed and then emitted a low growl.

Stormy and the kids were far enough inside that if they made a move to escape, the cougar would have plenty of time to attack.

Riggs readied his gun as he tugged Honey off to

the side of the cave opening and moved in front of the others, providing a human barrier. He couldn't leave them, but the horse would kick and put up a fight if forced closer to the feline. Too dangerous. With no other choice, he let the horse go. Honey darted from the cave and into the storm, kicking her back legs into the air.

Now they were all alone with a trapped mountain lion. Stormy held on to Kay-Kay and Jonah while backing them deeper into a crevice, over to the side and away from the opening. He didn't want to shoot the animal, but he'd do anything to protect this woman and kids.

Losing another child was out of the question.

The cougar crouched and readied to pounce.

Stormy's hands shook as she kept the light on the wild cat. They had intruded on his territory, but there was simply no other place to go. Kay-Kay desperately clung to Stormy's leg.

Without warning, Shotgun darted around to the back of the cave and exploded into a barking frenzy.

"Come, Shotgun," Riggs commanded. The Australian shepherd ran to him but continued to bark, his hackles raised.

The cougar let out another scream.

A shiver of fear went up Stormy's spine, and she handed Jonah to Kay-Kay. The baby cried. She shoved them deeper into the corner while using her body to stand between them and the cat.

Riggs yelled, "Stay back!"

In a quick movement, the cat leaped and struck out with his claw, striking Stormy across the arm.

A shot exploded in the confined area.

A shrill scream, and then the cat bounded from the cave opening and disappeared.

Blood ran down her bicep, and pain mushroomed through her arm. She clasped the wound with her other hand, trying to stop the bleeding.

"Are you all right?" Riggs was beside her in a second.

"Yes. I think so." Her body shook uncontrollably.

Kay-Kay's lips puckered. "I want to go home."

"I know, baby," Riggs said tenderly. "We'll take you home soon."

Jonah bawled hysterically.

Stormy watched a conflicted expression cross Riggs's face as his brows drew in, even as she continued to apply pressure to her arm. They needed to get the kids to safety. There was no time for injuries.

"Let me see." Riggs indicated her arm. When she hesitated, he moved closer. "I know the cougar got you. I need to examine it."

She shook her head. "I'm fine."

"Stormy. It's okay." His dark eyes found hers, and their gazes locked. "I'm here to help."

Against her better judgment, she allowed him to move her hand away from her bicep.

He let out a whistle as he turned her arm to get a better look. "He got you good. We need to get something around that to stop the bleeding." Without hesitation, he removed his thin Western shirt and white T-shirt. Quickly, he put his shirt back on and buttoned it halfway up. "I'm afraid my shirt is too dirty to use as a bandage but hopefully my undershirt is clean enough."

She slumped against the damp rock and leaned her

head against the wall. Shotgun moved to her side and sniffed her, seemingly aware of the situation.

Riggs ripped his cotton shirt into strips. "Get back, Shotgun."

The dog went and stood beside the kids. Jonah's cries continued but not quite as loudly. Shotgun circled the children and lay down in front of Kay-Kay, his tail thumping against the floor. Jonah immediately grew quiet.

She watched Riggs, noting his muscular arms but the gentle touch of his hands as he wrapped the soft fabric around the wound. The action stung, but she held herself still against the pain while he tenderly tied off the ends.

"There. That should stop the bleeding and keep it clean." He ducked to get a better look into her eyes. "Are you okay?"

His nurturing caused a lump to form in her throat. She wasn't used to being coddled, or at least she thought she wasn't. Leaning on others had never been her forte, because it gave them access to hurt you. Exhaustion must have taken over her good sense, for his unexpected actions were making her emotional, and she fumbled for the right response. She settled for her go-to reply. "I'm fine."

"Sorry if the bandage is tight. We need to stop the bleeding. As soon as we are out of the canyon, we'll find medical care."

"That may not be necessary. The bleeding has already slowed. A little antibiotic and I should be as good as new. I'm more concerned with getting Kay-Kay and Jonah to safety." She had been in worse situations before. She didn't take time to question how she knew that.

Even though the cloth was snug and caused her arm to throb, she swallowed back the pain.

He drew a deep breath and climbed to his feet. The frustration in his expression was obvious. "Sorry to let you down. I should've shot the animal when I first saw her."

"What? No. You had the children to think about." Then she wondered about the cougar. "Did you hit it?"

"No. I shot above its head."

"I'm glad. And no wonder the horses didn't want to come in here."

"I agree. The animals have a better sense of danger than we do. I totally misread their warning." Riggs held up his finger. "Let me see how deep the cave is and make certain there are no more animals in here."

Shotgun leaped to his feet and ran alongside Riggs. The man appeared none too happy they'd tried to force the horses inside. She, too, had assumed the animals were just afraid of the storm.

Kay-Kay got up and moved beside Stormy and stared at the bandage. "Does it hurt?"

"Only a bit." She held out her hands. "I'll take Jonah now."

After the boy was seated on Stormy's leg on the opposite side of her injury, Kay-Kay's small fingers stroked the cotton, a frown firmly in place. "The cat was big and scary. I did not like him."

Stormy smiled. "Me neither, but I think we invaded his home."

Kay-Kay's mouth dropped open. "We did?"

Stormy nodded. "Yes. But the gunshot scared him away. We need to keep our distance from him."

"I will."

Riggs returned a minute later. "The cave goes back another twenty feet, but it grows narrower. It may be small, but I think we're better off staying in this main room until the storm is over."

"I agree. We can't see well anyway until the rain lets up. Let's hope the gunmen aren't able to move easier than we are."

Kay-Kay continued to stare at her arm. "I cut my finger on a piece of glass, and my daddy put a princess Band-Aid on it." She turned her hand to show Stormy. "On this one. Or maybe it was this one."

Stormy grinned at the sweet girl. She could only imagine Kay-Kay's pain and confusion of missing her family.

Would they ever make it to the top of the ridge to call for help? Now the injury would only delay them.

Riggs glanced around. "There's not enough wood or brush to start a fire." He strode to the cave opening and watched as the rain continued. The lightning appeared to be moving farther away.

She sighed. "That's okay. We shouldn't be staying long." She repositioned Jonah in her lap, careful not to hurt her right arm.

Kay-Kay ran over to Riggs and held her hands into the air. "Hold me."

The cowboy didn't hesitate to scoop her up. He ran his hands along her arms. "You're freezing."

"And wet." A giggle laced Kay-Kay's voice. Her long, curly hair matted against her head, making Stormy want to brush out the tangles and pull it back with barrettes. Her turquoise T-shirt brought out the blue of her eyes. No doubt, she'd be cute as a bug once cleaned up.

Riggs was patient with the kids, not seemingly an-

noyed with their chatter or constant needs. A rare trait
for certain.

"Since we're here, we might as well have something
to eat." She dug into her backpack and pulled out the
box of the breakfast bars. The box was wet, but the foil
packaging kept the food dry. She held one out to each
Kay-Kay and Riggs.

Riggs shook his head. "I'm not hungry."

She cocked her head. "Are you certain? You might
not get another opportunity for a while."

"Eat it." Kay-Kay looked up at him. "It's for you."

His mouth twisted up. "Okay. You talked me into it."

Stormy dug out a small baggie of dog food from her
backpack and dumped it on the ground. The dog went to
work devouring the food, his tail wagging a steady beat.

Except for Shotgun crunching on the kibble, they all
ate in silence as the storm raged outside. As much as she
was ready to keep going so they could get cell reception,
it felt good to get off her feet. Now that her arm was
hurt, she was determined not to slow them down. They
simply had to keep moving, no matter how she felt.

She'd guess it was early afternoon, but it was difficult to tell with the dark clouds. She didn't know how
many hours she'd been awake. "How long do you think
it'll take to reach the old home place from here?"

He shrugged. "Another hour because of the rain,
depending on how fast we can travel. Much depends
on how many temporary rivers we must cross. Flash
floods are common, but not this high up." Riggs's eyes
connected with hers. Even in the dark shadows, she
could see the intenseness. "Have you remembered anything else?"

"Not really. It's weird. I have feelings about my past, but not clear memories."

"Like what?"

"I don't know how to explain, but I'll try. I think I got these kids from somewhere nearby. I don't feel like I did anything illegal, but like maybe I'm in law enforcement." She was hesitant to admit her next thought. "I just hope it's not wishful thinking, and that I wasn't involved in something I shouldn't have been."

He stared at her. "What kind of law enforcement? FBI, maybe?"

Okay. That was a specific question. "Could be. More like I'm on a mission."

Riggs looked down at Kay-Kay. "Where is your mama?"

Stormy held her breath. She could've asked the girl that question much earlier but wasn't sure she wanted to hear the answer.

The little girl shrugged. "I dunno. Probably work."

Inwardly, Stormy smiled at the girl's demeanor. "Where does your mama work?"

"The store."

If Kay-Kay were only a little older, she'd be able to communicate better. Stormy tried to keep the questions simple. "Do you know the name of the store?"

"No. Just the store. Sometimes Mama brings me home a surprise."

"Like a hamburger and fries?"

The girl giggled like that was the funniest thing ever. "No. Not a burber. Sometimes candy or a lollipop."

Okay. It sounded like her mom worked at a convenience store, or a place that sold groceries—maybe even a big-box store. None of that sparked a memory.

Riggs shot Stormy a look before he continued. "What about your daddy?"

"Daddy?" She giggled.

He continued, "Do you have a daddy?"

"I got a new daddy." She beamed and then proudly added, "Me and Jonah stay with Uncle Matt, too, sometimes until Mama gets home. Mama gets mad because she says we watch too much TV over there and eat too much pizza."

"That's fine, honey." Stormy shot Kay-Kay a smile. It sounded like their parents were divorced, or maybe were never married and her mom had just married for the first time.

Riggs whispered, "I was just trying to find out if she could tell us more. If we knew who her folks were, maybe we could learn who was after us."

"Why don't we wait until we contact the authorities and get help? We can go to the address in Amarillo and see who is there. Maybe it's the address to their parents' house."

Riggs frowned. "Someone is trying to kill us. We need to know."

"Fine. But let me ask the questions."

He swung an open-palmed hand across his body as if saying *go ahead.*

"Kay-Kay bug, how did you get out here?"

"You brought me."

Stormy smiled, afraid the girl misunderstood. "Did I take you from your mama?"

The girl frowned. "No, that bad man did."

Whew. That was a relief. "Do you know his name?"

Kay-Kay shook her head and shrugged. "I don't remember." She scowled. "They made me and Jonah cry. I didn't like him. He was not nice."

Stormy scooted closer. "This is important because I'm having a hard time remembering. I hope you can help me."

Her head cocked sideways. "I'm a good helper."

"Yes, you are." Stormy laughed at the girl's honesty. "Where did you first see me?"

"What?" Her face wrinkled up.

How to phrase the question so Kay-Kay would understand? She drew a deep breath. "Where did I find you?"

Her lips pressed together. "At the big house with all the people."

She exchanged glances with Riggs before turning her attention back to Kay-Kay. "What people, honey?"

"The kids. And Tami. Tami was nice. She held me when I was crying."

Riggs leaned forward. "Was Tami a kid?"

"No." Kay-Kay giggled. She stretched her hand high into the air. "Tami is big."

"Did you know Tami before the bad man took you from your mama?"

Her eyebrows knitted. "No." She sighed and then got up and moved closer to Stormy and laid her head down on her leg. "I want to go home now."

Stormy rubbed her back and stared across at Riggs. "Do you think the kids were kidnapped?"

"That's exactly what I was thinking." His jaw clenched. "And whoever is behind it can't afford for us to learn the truth. That makes Kay-Kay our best witness."

Would the girl be able to pick out her kidnapper from

a lineup? She was awfully young. And would the people at the holding house be willing to chance a four-year-old who could identify them? Not only were Stormy's life and Riggs's life in danger, but Kay-Kay might be the next target.

SIX

Worry sat heavily on Riggs's shoulders, weighing him down. Even though the rain had slowed, they still had a long trek to the old house. The horses were gone, and Stormy was injured.

The idea of separating was out of the question, even though it would be faster if he climbed to the rim while Stormy stayed with the kids. By himself, he could climb almost straight up instead of winding up the safe trail. Stormy had a gun for protection should the cougar or the gunmen return. The cave kept them out of the rain, and it prevented Kay-Kay from having to walk anymore. Poor child was bound to be worn out.

He glanced out across the canyon. The rain had almost stopped, and the sun had come out, casting a bright reflection against puddles and wet rock. Stormy had not complained about her injury, but she wasn't fooling him. The cut needed stitches, and he had nothing to sew it up with. If she bumped it wrong, or they were attacked again, the wound could reopen and start bleeding even more. The cut must be painful, and she was trying to be brave. The longer he spent with the woman, the more he respected her. At first he hadn't bought her amnesia story, but he believed her more as time went on. It was apparent she had received training. She would've made a great addition to the FBI team.

He glanced back at the woman. She had moved the children deeper into the cave and rested with them now. The baseball cap she normally wore lay on the ground, allowing her hair to cascade across her shoulders. As he approached, Shotgun looked up, and his tail thumped against the cave floor.

Stormy's eyes opened, and she blinked the sleep away.

He knelt close to her side. When she started to get up, his hand went to her shoulder, and he whispered, "No, no. Stay where you are. Rest. The kids are exhausted. The rain has nearly stopped. We'll be ready to go after their nap."

"If it's through storming, now would be a good time hike to the rim." She shoved her hair away from her face, but a stubborn stray piece still dangled against her cheek.

He couldn't resist moving the stray hair with his fingers behind her ear.

A softness crossed her face, but she didn't respond.

She kept her voice down. "Why don't you go to the rim, and I'll stay here with the kids. You can make better time by yourself."

The argument made sense, but the answer was still no. "We can't chance it, Stormy. The cougar could return, but I'm more worried about Waylon and Sonny. We don't know where they are. I'm hoping they're hunkered down somewhere because of the rain, or they could be watching this place, just waiting for the opportunity to move."

"They could be gone by now."

"Do you believe that?"

"Not really. But it's possible."

He grinned. At least she was honest. He wished he could make the trip by himself. He could be there and back in half the time.

"We'll be fine. Go. I have two guns and ammo."

"I won't take the chance."

She stared at him. Her face turned into a frown, and it looked like she wanted to argue.

"Trust me, Stormy. I want to call for help as much as you, but it won't do any good if one or both of us get taken out."

"Okay." She released a breath. "I can make it. I'll keep up."

"I know you won't slow us down." His gaze went to her arm, where the cougar had slashed her. Red showed through the fabric, indicating it had continued to bleed. "Finish resting, and we'll go as soon as you're ready."

Instead of staying put, she climbed to her feet and put her cap back on.

"What are you doing?"

"I can carry Jonah if you take Kay-Kay."

"We need to make certain the bleeding has stopped. I don't mind waiting."

"And give the gunmen more time to find our trail? No way."

Riggs didn't like it, but he agreed as long as it didn't put her in danger. Stormy changed Jonah and took Kay-Kay potty while he repacked the backpack and checked the guns. Within ten minutes, they were ready to leave.

"Let me have Jonah." Riggs held out his hands.

Stormy shook her head. "I can manage."

He took the boy from her anyway. She didn't need the extra stress on her arm. "I don't mind." Jonah fit perfect in the crook of his arm, and the little fellow looked up at him with trusting brown eyes. "We get along just fine, don't we, pardner?"

A toothless grin rewarded Riggs. They all walked away from the cave and down the trail with Shotgun at their feet.

As soon as they were on level ground, below the cave, Stormy looked around. "Which way is the nearest town?"

"North." Was she thinking of leaving and heading out on her own? "Do you know which way that is?"

"Yes." With the cave to her back, she pointed in front of her. "That is west—" she pivoted to the right "—so that way is north."

"Correct. Just so you know, the closest town is fifteen to eighteen miles north on the county road. Traffic is virtually zilch out here, but someone could come along. It'd be dangerous to attempt that trek with the kids and without me."

She frowned. "I wouldn't go off unless you were injured. Plan A is to walk to the old place you mentioned and call the sheriff's department. But if you get hurt or something, I need a backup strategy."

Did she have ulterior motives? The thought of her being out here alone with the kids scared him to death. Nothing would knock him out of commission—he'd see to it.

Sprinkles hit him, and he pulled his Stetson lower to provide more protection as they headed toward the large uphill climb up the canyon. A faint trail spread out in front of them, and he moved onto it. Before he headed up, he turned and gave one glance back. Nothing moved. But that didn't mean the men weren't out there, ready to strike while he and the small group were the most vulnerable.

The heel of his boot slipped on the rock, sending his foot in front of him. "Whoa." He regained his balance. "Be careful and try to step on the dirt and avoid the stone if possible."

"I understand. Glad I'm wearing my hiking boots."

Noticing Kay-Kay was struggling to keep up, he threw her on his shoulders with one hand while the other held Jonah. The girl squealed with delight.

"At least let me carry your hat."

He handed the Stetson to Stormy. Having both kids with him gave him a funny feeling—made him aware of what was at stake. He didn't know where Stormy had found the kids, but he'd do everything in his power to get them home to their parents. He tried to take the easiest route possible that would also be quick, an impossible task. When he'd gone about a hundred yards, he turned and looked back down again. The cave was no longer in sight.

He continued up the side of the hill, taking long strides, and Stormy kept pace. The rain had stopped, and a heavy mugginess replaced the cool temperatures. It'd feel good to get out of the grungy clothes and into something clean. He removed his cell phone from his pocket and checked the bars. Still nothing. Not that he'd believed there would be a signal, but he wanted to get the call made as soon as possible.

Fifteen minutes later, he stood beside the lone tree at the rim and checked his phone again. Nothing. He'd been afraid of that with the storms but still found it frustrating. The next higher rim he'd been aiming for sat straight across the valley. A huge flat stone was near the top, and he set that as his next target. They'd made good time so far and started down the other side.

Birds soared in the sky above, and his clothes stuck to him. His soaked boots caused his foot to rub against the leather, but nothing was going to slow him down. As he trudged across the valley, he continued to check his surroundings. The rain would keep the dust down if the men returned in their truck, so he needed to be extra vigilant. The good thing was it would be too muddy for a truck to travel across the open areas.

The way the men had blown up his house continued to play through his mind. They had backing—money. Who came prepared with that kind of firepower for a woman and two kids?

If he hadn't heard the gunshots, would the gunmen have simply shot Stormy and taken the kids? It would've been easy. Whatever she had witnessed was no trivial matter.

He didn't know how she'd escape them, but Stormy must've put up a good fight to get as far as she had. They hadn't come across a vehicle yet. How many miles had she traveled with two kids?

He turned to look at Stormy, and a shadow moved down below them. "We've got company."

Stormy glanced over her shoulder. Sure enough, someone moved behind a juniper tree. The distance was near a hundred yards, but with her injured arm and Riggs carrying the children, it shouldn't take long for the man to close the gap. She removed her gun from the backpack and clicked the safety off. "Go on. I'll keep him away."

"No doing," Riggs said. "You come with us."

"I know how to use a gun, but I can't carry the children."

"You can shoot with your left hand?"

"I can manage. There's no choice." Her gaze continued to search the landscape for the other gunman. Last night, the two had separated. She spoke over her shoulder. "Have you spotted the other man?"

"No. And not the pickup, either."

The man darted from behind the tree and zigzagged from the bushy cover up the canyon toward them. From here, the man looked like Sonny, the heavier man, not Waylon.

Riggs slid Kay-Kay from his shoulders and held out Jonah. "Take the baby and keep your weapon with you. Kay-Kay can walk quickly with your help. But my gunfire will slow the man down. Look for a shelter or any good hiding place. I'll find you."

Stormy knew she was good with weapons, but Riggs was right. She wouldn't be as accurate with her left hand. Not wasting time, she took Jonah in her left arm and headed straight up the hill.

"Shotgun, go with them."

The Australian shepherd took off and caught up quickly. She trusted the dog to warn them if the other gunman was nearby. Kay-Kay struggled to keep pace, and Stormy slowed so the girl would not fall and injure herself. "You're doing good, Kay-Kay."

Her face wrinkled up. "Are those bad men chasing us again?"

"One of them is."

"I don't want them to catch us."

"They won't. Riggs is watching out for us." Even as she said the words, she knew it was true. The cowboy would protect them.

Kay-Kay's shoe hit the mud, and she fell to her knees. She cried and attempted to stand back up. Shotgun licked her face.

"Take your time, honey. I'll wait on you." Using her injured arm, she stuck her hand out to help her. Pain shot through her bicep as Kay-Kay tugged her hand to get back to her feet. Stormy cringed but forced herself to be patient. Even though Stormy desired to move faster, it wasn't fair to the girl. She didn't want to scare the kids—if need be, they'd hunker down and she would shoot at the assailant. As they moved again along the rim, she searched for a good place to hide.

Gunfire exploded behind them. Stormy turned to see Riggs shooting, as the man was within fifty yards. Shotgun barked.

"Stay," she commanded.

Kay-Kay covered her ears. "I don't like this! Make it stop!"

They needed to move! "Come on." Keeping a watch for the other gunman, they hurried down the other side, out of sight of Riggs. Down at the bottom of the canyon in the valley was a long crevice where a small river ran fast from the rains. Dark shadows dotted the area, and she hoped it was large boulders or even another cavity or cave.

More gunfire echoed through the canyon. A sudden rumbling of an engine sounded to her right.

The maroon truck raced across the rim.

"Keep going." Stormy forced her voice to be calm.

"Go!" Riggs shouted from behind them. "I've got you covered."

Stormy glanced over her shoulder to see Riggs running toward them, but his attention was on the truck. He aimed his weapon and fired three quick shots. The truck's back window exploded.

The dog barked at Riggs but continued running beside them.

"Come on, Shotgun." She grabbed Kay-Kay's hand, even though pain exploded throughout her body. The little girl sobbed as Stormy led her around the far side of the bushes. Jonah's eyes were wide, his lip puckered, but he didn't make a sound. He looked ready to burst into a bawling fit.

An enormous boulder appeared about thirty yards in front of them, and Stormy moved toward it. The rock must've been one of the dark shadows she'd seen earlier. "We're almost there," she said to the girl.

Kay-Kay didn't answer but slowed her pace.

The rev of the engine and sounds of tires spinning gave Stormy hope the gunman was stuck. As they neared the boulder, the ground opened up with a large crack and grew deeper. The flash flood had caused a narrow but fast river in the canyon valley.

Just as Stormy reached the boulder, Kay-Kay screamed. Panting for breath, Stormy fell against the rock and turned to the girl, planning on hiding her behind the rock until the shooting was over.

But the four-year-old was gone.

Stormy's lungs froze as her gaze roamed the area. Panic surged. "Kay-Kay!"

"Help me!" Terror filled the tiny voice.

She repositioned Jonah on her arm and hurried toward the cry.

Riggs ran down the incline and reached her just as she came to the crevice. He huffed. "The gunmen are gone for now. Where's Kay-Kay?"

A glance to Kay-Kay's shoe, next to a jagged and slender crack in the ground, had Stormy's heartbeat racing, nearly exploding. She dropped to her knees and shoved her hand into the hole, feeling for the girl. Pain shot up her injured arm, but she kept searching, finding nothing except for rock and air. Her voice trembled. "She fell through the crack. Down there."

Riggs called into the hole. "Kay-Kay bug, are you in there?"

"Yes," she cried.

"Hold on, we'll get you out."

But Stormy could tell from where she stood, the crevice was too narrow for either of them to crawl through. They had to get the girl out. Kay-Kay's sobs sent chills down her spine.

They must hurry before the gunmen came back.

SEVEN

Water trickled into the crevice, but most of the flow ran along the other side of the crevice and deeper into the valley. Stormy watched as Riggs bent over and grabbed the rock.

He said, "Get back, I'll get her." With a jerk, he tried to loosen the slab. Defined muscles twitched in his arms as he strained against the much-too-heavy stone. A paltry chunk broke off, and he stumbled backward before regaining his balance.

Please, Lord, help us get Kay-Kay out.

As she cradled Jonah in her arm, she watched with fascination as Riggs worked to free Kay-Kay. She couldn't know for certain, but she felt as though she'd met no one like the cowboy before. He was caring and willing to his put his life on the line to save a stranger and two small children. What kind of man did that?

Kay-Kay called up. "Are you going to get me out?"

He stopped and put his hands on his hips and let out a big breath. "Yes, darling. Don't worry. I'm going to get you out of that hole no matter how long it takes."

"Good," she whined. "I don't like it down here. I'm afraid in the dark."

Riggs turned to Stormy. "Do you still have your flashlight?"

"Yes." She dug it from her pocket and handed it to him.

He hollered down into the hole, "Kay-Kay, I'm going to give you a flashlight. Stand back." Riggs clicked on the device and reached down as far as he could before letting go. A clattering sounded. "Can you get that?"

"Yes. I can see." Excitement filled her voice.

"Okay. You're doing good." He went back to work, trying to pry up another stone. It barely budged, much of the stone wedged under another rock.

Stormy said, "I wished we had a metal rod or a sturdy limb to pry it up."

"Me, too." He continued to work even as he spoke.

Shotgun moved to the edge of the hole and barked. Using his paws, he clawed at the hard surface but couldn't penetrate the ground. He barked again.

"Shotgun?" Kay-Kay's voice carried up.

"The dog is here," Riggs called down.

"Aw. I wished he could come down here with me."

Riggs turned to Stormy.

"What if the dog gets down there, and then we can't get him out? Do you really want to take that chance?"

His lips flattened. "You're right. I'm sure the fellow would comfort her, but I don't want to make matters worse."

Stormy's heart went out to him as he let Kay-Kay know Shotgun couldn't go. The cowboy took the little girl's fear to his soul. When the explosion destroyed his home, Riggs had barely mentioned it. The loss must've bothered him, so how could he not complain? Respect for the man grew. When all this was over, Stormy was going to owe him.

Overwrought with exhaustion, she leaned against the boulder and slid to the ground with Jonah still in her grip. The baby was awake but quiet. He was such a delightful baby. Some babies naturally were, while others were a ball of constant movement and energy. She couldn't help but wonder if Jonah was normally more active.

Her arm throbbed, and when she checked the bandages again, she noticed the cotton was seeping through with blood. She had hoped she wouldn't need stitches, but right now that was out of the question.

Jonah touched her face and tugged the hair that had fallen out of the cap. She grinned at him.

She glanced to the horizon for signs of the gunmen but saw nothing. "I heard gunfire. Was anyone injured?"

For a moment Riggs didn't answer, and she wondered if he'd heard her. Finally, he paused his work. "I shot the man on foot. I think it was Sonny, the big guy. He dropped, but I don't know if he survived. I didn't wait around to check it out."

The man in the truck had driven away, so there was no reason to inquire about him. Did he go back for his partner?

Fifteen minutes later, Kay-Kay had become quiet, and Riggs's breath came in bursts. He was tiring fast. What if they couldn't get her out? Or what if another storm came through and flooded the hole? She couldn't take it anymore. "Give me a turn."

She tried to hand Jonah to Riggs, but the man shook his head. "It's no good. You're strong, but you don't have the weight for leverage. There's no need for both of us to be exhausted."

"What are we going to do?" she whispered so Kay-Kay wouldn't overhear. "We can't leave her down there."

"I would never leave her. Never." The annoyance in his voice surprised Stormy. He looked around, surveying the land. "There's got to be another way. You mentioned a metal rod. My fence has T-posts, but it's not close."

"I could go find one while you work on this."

"We are not going to separate. Period." He sighed. "There's got to be a better way. How big did the hole look to you?"

"If you're asking if I can fit down there, I can't. I'd never get both legs in."

"If I held your feet, could you get your arms far enough in to reach her?"

Stormy had thought of that earlier. "I don't know, but I'm willing to try anything. We have to get her out."

Riggs pulled his cell phone out of his pocket and hit a couple of buttons.

"Anything?"

He shook his head and shoved it back into his jeans. "Didn't think it'd hurt to try again. If we just had help— It'd be easy to get this rock up if we had tools."

"Okay. Let's try it." She was careful to make sure where she put Jonah on the ground had no rocks that were choking size. At this point, staying clean or eating a little dirt was not a concern, but she brushed away small pebbles so they wouldn't hurt his knees, anyway. Shotgun trotted over to the boy and lay down beside him. Jonah's face instantly broke into a grin, and he cooed.

Riggs took a deep, pained breath and closed his eyes. A moment later, they blinked open again as guilt played across his face. Thankfully, he said nothing and didn't argue about her going into the opening, although he probably wanted to.

She lay down on her stomach—careful of her injury—and then put her arms into the hole. When she stretched out full length, Riggs gripped her feet. Fear that he would drop her and that she'd hurt her gash flitted through her mind, but she had to trust him. "Okay. I'm ready."

He lifted her feet until her midsection dipped down, and her hands plunged into the cavity. Immediately, a large rock blocked her way. "Hold on." She wormed her way around it until her hands were free. "Try it again."

Her fingers searched out for Kay-Kay but felt nothing. The maze of rocks made it to where she couldn't see the girl. "Can you see my hands? Kay-Kay, try to grab me."

"All right." The little girl's voice came out shaky and tired, but at least she was trying. A grunt emitted from below, but she sounded too far away. "I can't."

"You can't quit. You can do this, sweetie. Is there a rock you can climb up?"

"No." Her voice turned to a cry. "I want out. I can't do it."

Stormy drew a deep breath. She had to reach Kay-Kay before she gave up. This was more dangerous than she first anticipated. "Riggs, I need to go deeper."

"There's not much room. I can't afford to lose my leverage. I'm pulling you out."

"No. I can almost reach her. We're so close. Let me try it again." She knew he was afraid of dropping her. If he let go, she would fall into the crevice, and then it would be almost impossible to rescue them without help. "Try it anyway. We're all exhausted, and this is going to get worse."

"Once more." An inch at a time, he lowered her down, allowing her to squirm her way around the obstacles. Finally, her arms dangled freely into the cavity. The space was much larger than she'd expected, and a glow illuminated in the bottom. "I'm in."

"Can you grab Kay-Kay?"

"I don't know." She carefully swung her arms, trying to find the little girl. "Shine the light on me, honey."

The girl turned the light directly on her face, blinding her, and Stormy turned away. "Point it at my hands."

"Okay." The beams wavered and then landed in the general direction of her arms.

Now that she could see, Stormy spotted a minor fracture in the slab that might offer the girl leverage. "Right there." Stormy pointed. "Do you see that crack at the bottom?"

"This?" Kay-Kay put her fingers in it.

"Yes." The blood rushed to Stormy's head, causing her head to swim with dizziness. She allowed the feeling to pass before she again stretched her arms out. "Put your shoe in the crack and grab my hands."

Kay-Kay did as Stormy asked, but her foot slid back down. After two more tries, the girl cried. "I want out of here."

"That's it."

Before Stormy had time to react, Riggs was pulling her back up, causing her to bump her elbow. "Ow."

"Sorry." As soon as she was out of the hole, he glanced at the cut. "Are you all right?"

She nodded. "I hit my funny bone. But I almost had her." She formed a *u* with her fingers. "I was this close."

"It's time we get that little girl out now."

"But—"

Riggs cut her off. "Stand back."

Frustration bit at her. After rescuing the children and being shot at by gunmen and Riggs's house being blown to smithereens, Kay-Kay falling in a hole was causing them the biggest hurdle.

Stormy glanced at Jonah to see him lying on his belly, watching them. Shotgun lay beside him with his tongue hanging out. She turned her attention back to Riggs as he got to his knees. "You won't fit."

"Watch me." Riggs's gaze connected with hers, a storm brewing in those dark eyes. "That little girl is scared, and I won't stand by another second until I at least try."

Kay-Kay's cries for help were more than Riggs could stand. He thrust his head into the hole, and immediately an outcropping blocked his progress. If Stormy could work her way in there, so could he, even if he was larger. Rock bit into his face, and he worked himself around the barrier. Once he was past, the crevice opened up.

Suddenly, something grabbed his ankles. He said, "Hey. I got it."

"You don't need my help?"

"No. Get back, Stormy. I don't want you to hurt your arm." He waited until she released her grip. He was glad for her help, but it made him more nervous worrying about hurting her. Besides, she'd never be able to hold his weight.

As he moved deeper in the hole, his calves brushed against the sides. A light shined in his eyes.

"Riggs!" Excitement laced the girl's tone.

"Hello, honey. Aren't you tired of playing down here?" His boots clung to the edge, and he had to dig them in so he wouldn't fall. One knee rested against a stone, and his left hand pushed against the wall to give himself leverage.

"I fell." Kay-Kay laughed. "I wasn't playing."

"Sure looks like it. Grab my hand." He held his right hand out.

The girl reached up, and her fingers brushed his. She grunted.

"Try again. You almost had it." She did as he asked, but he couldn't quite get a grip. "Stretch, honey, you got it."

She gave a mighty lunge for a four-year-old, and his hand grabbed hers. To make certain he didn't dislocate her arm, he swung his body at the waist for momentum and tossed her higher, grabbing her around her stomach for a secure grip. He pulled her against him.

She wrapped her arms around her neck and clung tight. A sudden relief filled him, but he couldn't stop now. He still had to get them back out. "Here we go."

"Okay," she said happily, like they were playing a game.

Using his left hand, he shoved himself upward and moved his legs a little back up the opening. Back and forth, he squirmed for better position while keeping a firm hold on Kay-Kay. She must've thought it was fun, for her smile remained plastered in place. It just went to show the trust kids had in adults.

Sweat dripped from his face and down his arms and

hands. It'd help if he could wipe his hands dry, but there was no way. Working to dig up the rocks had exhausted his muscles. No matter how hard he concentrated, he couldn't stop his arms from trembling.

Stormy called from above, "You're almost out. Is there anything I can do?"

Sweat dripped into his eyes, the salt burning them and causing him to blink. He grunted, "No. I got it."

Drawing three deep breaths, he powered himself backward using his knees, hand and torso. Now all he had left was the awkward angle around the rock near the entrance. "Hang on. We're almost out."

Twisting his body, he wiggled himself backward until his knees were firmly planted on the ground, and he emerged with Kay-Kay.

"I can't believe you did it," Stormy said. "I wouldn't have thought you would fit."

Shotgun licked his face.

Riggs leaned back and smiled. "Okay. Good boy. I'm fine."

Stormy attempted to pull the girl from his grasp, but he held on.

"I've got Macy Sue. Don't take her." His voice cracked against his will. For just a moment longer, he needed to hold the girl. The smell of her shampoo, the feel of the girl's arms around his neck, the knowing she was safe. He could feel Stormy's eyes on him, but he didn't care.

With everything in his power, he tried not to break down.

"Are you okay?" Stormy's voice breathed concern.

If only he could've saved his own daughter.

Kay-Kay twisted in his hold and said, "Let me down. I want to play with Shotgun."

Drawing a breath from deep in his chest, he gave the girl one last squeeze and put her feet on the ground. He watched as she ran to the dog, elated she was all right.

Suddenly, the skin on his calves burned, probably from scraping the side of the rock. "Any sign of the gunmen?"

Stormy held Jonah in her arms, a funny look on her face. "No. Nothing."

He looked up at her. "Let's get out of here while we can."

"Are you sure you're ready?" she whispered. "Do you need a break?"

"I need us to get cell reception and out of this canyon." He climbed to his feet, every muscle threatening to collapse. But they had to keep moving. If the gunmen returned to their home base and reloaded with bigger guns or recruited more men, he didn't want to be caught in the open again. They'd stayed alive so far, but he wasn't naive enough to believe they could keep stumbling their way out of danger.

Stormy stared strangely at him.

"What?" He asked.

"Who is Macy Sue?"

He frowned. "Where did you hear that name?"

"You called Kay-Kay that."

"That's ridiculous." He had no idea that had slipped out. Not wanting to answer any more question, he again put Kay-Kay on his shoulders and carried Jonah.

"I'm not helpless." Stormy glowered. "I can carry a baby."

"Humor me. Take care of your arm until we can get

you to an urgent care or hospital to stitch it up, and then I'll let you take care of me and the children."

Her eyes cut to him, questions still lingering. She finally said, "Hopefully, by then all the danger will be behind us."

"Exactly." He took off on the path leading up the gigantic hill in the canyon. It wasn't too much farther now, but it was a steep climb. Knowing Stormy wanted to do her share, he realized what a trooper she was and that she'd carry one of the kids, no matter how difficult. But he found it more beneficial to move quickly.

A glance back to her, and his heart softened. Despite the circumstances, he felt like he'd gotten to know her. Would things change as soon as they were rescued? Would she go her own way? Of course she would. Her life was somewhere else, although the amnesia was keeping her from remembering.

He didn't need to plan a relationship with the pretty redhead. They'd probably never see each other again.

Which was a pity, because he wouldn't mind staying in touch with her. They needed to keep their relationship purely about survival, nothing more. But he had the feeling he'd rather fight the cougar again than let her go.

EIGHT

Stormy couldn't quit thinking about Riggs calling Kay-Kay another girl's name. Who was Macy Sue? She had thought Riggs held secrets, but now she was more curious than ever. By the look he had shot at her, he didn't want to talk about it. That was fine, but she wouldn't forget about it.

Over the next thirty minutes, they hiked at a fast pace, only stopping once to give the kids and Shotgun a snack and a drink. With them getting closer to their destination, Stormy couldn't quit planning her next move. Check out the address in the backpack. Find her vehicle and figure out where she'd found Kay-Kay and Jonah. Which brought on thoughts about what Kay-Kay said about the big house with kids and people.

A vision formed in her mind of a large red farmhouse trimmed in white sitting among mesquite and willows a distance from the road. Cars were parked outside. Then there was an image of Kay-Kay holding Jonah outside behind some bushes.

But was Stormy simply imagining what the girl had described? Was her mind filling in what she thought might've occurred? Or was she remembering?

Blackness, too, seemed to rein her thoughts like impending doom. Dark shadows she couldn't escape.

Where did that overwhelming feeling come from? Something she'd witnessed, or a normal part of recovering from amnesia?

As she struggled to remember, her heart picked up pace, her shoulders drew taut and she found it difficult to breathe. But her mind refused to pull it to the surface. Stormy knew she might fill in what she wanted to know, but she didn't think so. She had seen something terrifying at the house when she found the kids.

Something her mind had blocked out.

But what? She'd rescued Kay-Kay and Jonah, so what triggered the reaction?

Fear raced through her even as she tried to bring it under control.

Fatigue didn't help her think clearly, and not knowing only made her imagination run amok with the worst-case scenarios.

What if she were part of the crime? Or maybe she'd witnessed terrible transgressions against children—the thought unbearable. Or could she have saved more kids but decided not to? The news was full of horrifying stories, and she couldn't help but worry about what Kay-Kay and Jonah had gone through.

She drew a deep breath. *Please, God, help me turn this situation over to You. Teach me to trust You and lean not on my own ways but know You'll see me through.*

"Are you okay?"

She jumped as Riggs's voice cut through her thoughts. "Yeah. I'm fine."

His eyes sliced to her, and she glanced away, not

wanting him to pick up on her doubt. Riggs was one thing in her current situation she was happy for. Without his help, she couldn't have survived.

It wasn't just how he related to her, but the kids. She could see the tenderness in his expression as he helped Kay-Kay out of the hole. He was determined. The way he took care of them spoke volumes. More caring than a lot of fathers. Riggs would make a wonderful daddy someday.

"Can you see it?" He pointed between the trees.

A decrepit house stood on the side of the hill—near the peak—and only a bit of white paint remained. One could easily miss the old home and walk right past. "Yeah, I do. I can just imagine the view from that point."

He nodded. "It's spectacular. I considered building my cabin there, but I wanted more level land for easier access to my ranch."

Losing his cabin plagued her with guilt. "What will you do about your home? Rebuild?"

"Probably," he answered. "I haven't thought about it much. There are things more important than a house and car." He cleared his throat. "The barn and utilities remain, so that's good. When I get on a case, I tend to get absorbed and put on blinders to the world around me. I will plan and worry it about it later."

Surprise shook her. "On a case? Like you're a law enforcement officer?"

"Shotgun, come." He snapped his fingers.

The dog had barely strayed. Was Riggs avoiding the question? It made sense, though. Of course, she should've known he'd received training. "What agency?"

He sighed. "The FBI. But I'm no longer with the bureau."

Disappointment slammed into her that he'd kept her in the dark. She'd thought they'd become close the past day. How silly of her. Her cheeks burned with heat, and she folded her arms. "You didn't think that was important to tell me earlier?"

"I thought you'd be glad." He held his hands up and shrugged.

"Happy you kept your experience a secret?" She scowled. "Did you have amnesia, too?"

He chuckled. "Of course not. It's not like I lied to you. But I wanted to reassure you if we find the other kidnapped children, you can trust me. I'm trained."

She heaved a deep, audible breath. "I'm not certain I do trust you, Riggs. You've had plenty of time to tell me your background while we were running amok on your ranch, trying to stay alive. Even though I had no memories, I *felt* like I was in law enforcement, felt the need to protect. I put a lot of pressure on myself because I thought you were a rancher who had no experience in situations like this."

"You're right. I should've told you."

The thing was, she did feel better knowing he had training, but not that he'd kept his past from her. What was she saying? She didn't know her own past.

Riggs wished he'd never mentioned putting on blinders or admitted to being an FBI agent. What purpose did it serve? The instant the words were out, he'd seen the hurt in her eyes. "Stormy, I'm sorry. I probably should've mentioned—"

Her hand shot up, palm toward him. "Not necessary

to apologize. You owe me nothing." Her steps were long and determined, like she was on a mission to get to the rim and out of this canyon. That *was* their mission, but it hadn't been because she'd wanted to escape *him*.

As they approached the house, Kay-Kay beamed. "A swing!"

A rusty swing set sat by the corner of the house surrounded by weeds. He glanced at Stormy again, wishing he'd kept his mouth shut.

"Hold on, Kay-Kay bug." He swung her from his shoulders and put her feet on the ground. "There could be snakes and bees and spiders in the tall grass. Don't go running in there."

Her eyes grew round, and her lip quirked up into a snarl. "I don't like spiders."

Stormy marched to the house and gave the steps a test before ascending the wooden boards. A screen door hung askew on its hinges and sagged against the porch. She stepped over a plastic bucket and flung the door open.

He started to warn her to be careful but didn't figure she needed to be told. He looked at Kay-Kay. "Stay here."

The girl nodded in agreement.

Shotgun had his nose to the ground, sniffing the variety of smells, his tail wagging vigorously. A jackrabbit darted from under the brush, and the dog's ears stood at attention, but he didn't give chase. After the long-eared fluff ball disappeared, he continued his mission of smelling his surroundings.

Riggs trekked through the grass to the swing, keeping an eye out for hazards. Surprisingly, the space was empty except for a few rotting branches that lay hidden among the tall weeds. Before he gave her the okay, he checked around the metal poles of the play set for bees' nests but found none. "Come on. You can play."

She ran to the swing and wormed her way into the seat. Besides needing a jump start, she was able to kick her legs and keep the motion moving. Riggs glanced down at Jonah. He was too young to join in the fun, but he seemed content watching his big sister.

"It's all clear." Stormy returned to the porch. "The house is not as bad as what I imagined."

Uncertain how to make amends, he kept the conversation simple. "Good. I'll see if I can make that call now."

She stepped over and took Jonah without a word.

He strode to the highest point above the old home, about forty yards away, with his cell phone in his grip. Though he was relieved Stormy and the kids were all right, he still didn't know how much longer they could hold out. *Please, let me get reception this time.*

He glanced at the screen. Two bars. He drew a deep breath and hit dial. With the cell phone to his ear, the buzz of a ring finally sounded after a couple of seconds.

"Sanderson County Sheriff's Department."

Riggs relaxed. "I need to speak with Sheriff Ludlam."

"May I tell him who's speaking?" the youthful, almost timid, female voice inquired.

He gave his name and prepared for a response in case she put him off, but she didn't.

"Sherriff Ludlam," the man answered.

Riggs's brief explanation was met with uninterrupted silence. When he was through, the sheriff responded, "Let me get this straight. Your lady friend has amnesia?" The word came out incredulous. "And someone is trying to kill you two and the children?"

Riggs tried not to get frustrated, as he'd half expected this reaction. "Yes, sir. We need help."

"I seriously doubt we have any kind of kidnapping ring in our county." After a grumble, the sheriff said, "I'll send one of my deputies out to look things over and the damage caused from the explosion. But I'll need you to come in and file a report."

Riggs gave him directions to the back entrance of his ranch and clicked off the phone. He hiked back down the hill to where Stormy waited. "A deputy is on the way."

A small smile crossed her lips. "Thanks."

"Do you need anything? Water?"

She shook her head. "Just letting the kids relax a bit. They've been put through the wringer."

They had been through a tough time, especially with Kay-Kay falling in the hole. He took a seat on the opposite end of the porch from Stormy, giving her space where he could keep an eye out for the deputy.

Shotgun would alert them if anyone approached, but Riggs kept his gun ready.

Stormy's neck ached when the sound of tires on gravel woke her. She hadn't planned on dozing, but the emotional stress had taken its toll. She squinted against the sun. A deputy's truck slowly came up the road.

Riggs turned toward her. "He's here. I've got the backpack ready to go."

She blinked as she tried to wake herself and climbed to her feet. "I'm ready."

A thirtyish deputy with dark wavy hair and a thick

mustache got out of the vehicle and strode their way. "Are you Riggs Brenner?"

"Yes, sir." Riggs shook his hand.

"Deputy Stan Jernigan. I barely made it through the canyon. The rain washed several places out." He looked them up and down, his gaze pausing on Stormy's crude bandage. "Sounds like y'all had a rough time of it."

"We sure did. She needs medical care." He jerked his head toward Stormy.

The deputy said, "Paramedics could meet us at the entrance to your ranch, or I can drop her off at Sanderson County Hospital."

Stormy said, "The hospital would be fine."

Riggs shoved his hands into his pockets. "Can my dog ride in the back of your truck?"

As if Shotgun understood, he wagged his tail and stared up at the deputy.

"I suppose so."

Riggs let down the tailgate and whistled. Shotgun leaped into the bed. With his front legs on the wheelbase and his tongue hanging out, he looked like he was ready to go.

Riggs motioned for Stormy. "Let's go."

Gladly. A few minutes later, all four of them sat in the truck with the deputy and headed down the rough path to the bottom of the canyon. Stormy had never felt so relieved in her life to be in a law enforcement vehicle. Much like the cavalry arriving during the old Western movies.

The children were quiet and in dire need of a bath, with dirt smudges on their cheeks and arms. Even though Stormy's hair was pulled back in a ponytail, after the rain and adventures, her hair could use a good washing. There's no telling how bad she looked. Automatically, she glanced at Riggs, sitting in the passenger seat, and couldn't help but notice how he didn't look so bad for all the mess they'd been through. His razor stubble was a little longer and his shirt untucked, but he still carried himself well.

The man was used to working outside. She might not have thought he was tired if it were not for the dark circles under his eyes. Even though bits and pieces of her memories had returned, she couldn't remember being this close to another man.

Why? Why had she stayed away from men? Sometimes the way Riggs looked at her suggested he found her attractive.

Or maybe she'd blocked out all romantic memories. Maybe she had been married before and it hadn't worked out. It did little good to ponder such things, but it was difficult to keep the thoughts at bay.

Twice the truck almost got stuck through a couple of washes and the deputy had to step on the gas. But after sliding sideways and keeping the accelerator down, they made it through. A while later, they were on the highway and headed west, the air-conditioning blowing her hair.

She laid her head back against the seat and watched out the window as the scenery whizzed by. The note with the address seemed to burn a hole in her backpack. She hoped the place contained a clue to her identity and where she'd found Kay-Kay and Jonah.

By the time they pulled into the emergency parking lot of the hospital thirty minutes later, the clock on the dash read three-thirty. It seemed so much later than that, like they'd been running for days. The tan brick building was old, and she wondered how good the staff would be. Thankfully, she only needed stitches. "You can rent a vehicle while I'm getting my arm looked at," she said to Riggs. "There's no need for you and the kids to wait on me."

"I don't mind sticking around."

She sighed. "You know how long these things can take. Just checking in can be thirty minutes…uh, I don't have any identification. Will they even see me?"

"I can vouch for you," the deputy said.

After the deputy stepped out of the vehicle, Riggs turned to her and said, "I don't like leaving you, but you're correct." He kissed her on the forehead like it was the most natural thing in the world. "I'll be right back, and we can go straight to the sheriff's department once you're done here."

"Good. I'll see you later, then." As much as she didn't want to admit it, she didn't enjoy seeing him go. That was silly. She was just vulnerable since she'd lost her memories. And maybe she shouldn't have allowed him to kiss her, even if it was only a peck. Was it such a bad thing, though, to be cared for?

She told the kids 'bye, and the deputy saw her to the front desk. Only one other person lingered in the waiting room—an older man with a walker standing in front of his chair. Deputy Jernigan explained the situation to the gray-haired woman behind the desk before he left.

The lady gave Stormy a form. She filled out all the information she could answer and then was ushered to a room. To her surprise, the hospital was clean and looked to have been recently updated.

After a few minutes of waiting, a lady sporting

Scooby-Doo scrubs entered her room. "Let's see what you have here." She cut off the bandage and washed the wound, and Stormy managed not to flinch when the antiseptic burned like fire. The nurse's gaze flitted to her. "Sorry. I know that must burn. How long ago were you injured?"

"About three or four hours ago."

She shook her head. "You should've come in earlier."

Stormy smiled. She could explain that coming in was out of her control but decided it wouldn't change anything now.

After the wound was clean and the nurse left the room, Stormy got a good look at the injury. Red and inflamed. It gaped open more than she realized. Kind of made her stomach churn to look at it, so she quit looking. After another twenty minutes of waiting, a female doctor in her thirties entered her room and closed the door.

"Hello. I'm Dr. Theresa Pitts." After a brief discussion, the physician stitched the wound and ordered a shot of antibiotic.

Stormy should tell the doctor about the amnesia but didn't want to spend the time in the hospital undergoing tests. Was that irresponsible? Probably. As the doctor was about to leave the room, Stormy said, "I have amnesia."

Dr. Pitts stopped dead in her tracks. "What makes you think that?"

Stormy explained how she awoke on the ledge. She kept the details light but included how a few memories had returned. "I'd rather not stay in the hospital, but I also don't want to take a chance with my health."

After a barrage of questions about how long she'd

had the memory loss and health questions that Stormy didn't know the answers to, the doctor asked, "Do you have any injuries besides the cut on the arm?"

"A bump on the head." Stormy touched the area.

The doctor examined her head. "Hmm. This doesn't look like a serious injury." She then tested her reflexes and had her walk across the office and perform simple balance and coordination exercises. "You appear healthy, but I'd need to perform a series of blood tests, cognitive tests and a CT scan or MRI to test for structural or functional lesions. It's impossible to tell by a visual examination. There are many things that can cause memory loss, from a stroke to low thyroid, emotional trauma and low vitamin B-12."

"I'm certain this is a recent problem, as in an injury. Can you give me an X-ray to rule out brain injury? That's my worst fear."

"A CT scan will show better images. If it comes back clear and the condition persists, you'll need to follow up with your doctor."

"That would be great."

Since it was a small hospital, the technicians got to her quickly. A little while later, the images were taken, and the doctor informed her the test showed no signs of injury.

When Stormy stepped out of the hospital with a prescription for an antibiotic and aftercare instructions, she looked for Riggs but didn't see anyone waiting around. There were no benches or place to sit, so she sat on the curb and waited. Even though she didn't think anyone would've followed her here, she kept a constant watch on her surroundings.

Ever since she had awakened on that ledge with amnesia, Riggs had been at her side. She realized she was looking forward to seeing him. As much as she felt safer having him near, she wondered at the wisdom of leaning on someone she'd just met.

Hopefully, she'd learn her identity soon and good things would follow. But what if she wasn't whom she believed herself to be? What if she had something incriminating to hide? She prayed this impending-doom feeling would pass.

NINE

A few minutes later, a black Ford pickup made the corner and came toward her. Riggs was driving, and she spotted the two kids and Shotgun in the back seat. He must've stopped somewhere and picked up child safety seats. The sight of Riggs sent butterflies to her stomach. Okay, now she was just being ridiculous. Yes, it felt good having him around, but it wasn't under normal circumstances. She had amnesia, and the constant danger had made her lean on him. Not to mention seeing him with children made her heart swell. No telling what she would've thought of him if she'd met him under different conditions.

That wasn't quite true. She fully believed she would like him anytime.

He pulled to a stop, and before she realized what he was doing, he'd gotten out and run to her side of the vehicle and opened the door for her.

"That's not necessary," she said. But inwardly she admitted she didn't mind.

"No problem. How are you feeling?"

She turned the bandage toward him. "Better. The

doctor deadened the area, so it wasn't painful. And just having it cleaned and stitched up makes me feel better."

"Good." He hurried back into the driver's seat. "Let's go make that report and see if the sheriff has learned anything."

"Does it hurt?" a little voice asked.

Stormy turned to see Kay-Kay's gaze on her bandage. "No. The doctor made it better."

The girl smiled. "Good."

Riggs drove across town with Kay-Kay talking up a storm and Jonah yelling unintelligible sounds. Shotgun seemed content to be back inside the cab again and with the children.

Fifteen minutes later, they pulled into the parking lot of the sheriff's department. They got out and strode into the station while Shotgun remained in the truck, but in view of the front room.

Deputy Jernigan glanced up from a corner desk, and a big man with gray hair came out of his office as soon as they stepped in, like he'd been waiting for their arrival. The man's gray eyes took them in. "Hello, folks. I'm Sherriff Rafe Ludlam."

Riggs introduced everyone to the sheriff.

"You look exhausted. Come on back and have a seat." The sheriff indicated the dark green cushioned chairs across from his desk. "Do you need something to drink? Water or a soda?"

"Water," Stormy and Riggs said in unison.

The sheriff smiled as he asked Deputy Jernigan to get them some bottles. He glanced to Riggs and held out a clipboard. "Since her hands are full, would you like to fill out the forms? She can add her part in a bit."

Stormy would be glad not to have to hold Jonah while

writing the information. Her arms weren't used to lugging a kid around all day. Hopefully, this wouldn't take long. Even though the water wasn't cold, it tasted refreshing to her parched throat. Kay-Kay was full of energy, and Jonah was getting restless and fussy.

After filling in most of the paperwork, Riggs handed the sheriff the several papers. "Come here, pardner." He exchanged Jonah for the clipboard. She quickly noted all the details she could recall—even her name, address and contact information were impossible to fill out.

When she was through, she handed the sheriff the papers. He'd been silently reading Riggs's documents and now sat quietly.

Riggs asked, "Have you had trouble with human trafficking around here? Or child abductions?"

The sheriff shook his head. "Nothing out of the ordinary. Most are relative abductions when families can't get along. There was a stranger abduction about six months back. The two men you describe would fit many people's description. But we'll check arrest records. If we can identify Waylon and Sonny, we can check it against descriptions in the other case. Come back tomorrow, and we'll try to have a possible suspects list."

"I'd appreciate that."

After they were done at the sheriff's office, they loaded back in the rented a four-door truck. It wasn't decked out quite as much as Riggs's vehicle, but it would still make it up and down the canyon with ease if needed.

They stopped off at the megastore and purchased a few more supplies—an extra set of clothes, toiletries and a charger for Stormy's cell phone.

She noticed Riggs kept a constant look at their surroundings and checked his rearview mirror often.

He glanced at her. "I'm ready to get to a hotel room and clean up."

"But I'd like to check out the address first. It could be important."

"I'm sure it is." He nodded. "But we're all exhausted and need a bath. If you're right and the address means something, then I want to be ready to go. Not dragging, and I need to be thinking clearly. Don't want to rush it and make a mistake."

Stormy didn't like it, but she agreed, since she felt filthy. Maybe a hot shower would clear her mind.

He handed her his cell phone. "Can you look up pet-friendly hotels?"

"Sure." A couple of minutes later, she gave him the names and addresses of what she'd found.

Riggs pulled into a moderately priced hotel. She waited in the truck with the kids while he went in a secured the room. When he returned, he pulled to the side near the front of the building.

"Is this a good place to park? Don't you think we should be at the back?"

"No one should know what we're driving." He looked at her. "And if they do, we're in trouble, anyway. I'd like to see the road and who comes and goes."

"Okay. I see your point."

Riggs lugged their purchases in while Stormy took Jonah, and Kay-Kay and Shotgun followed to their room, which was on the third floor. Riggs had rented a mini suite with two queen beds, a microwave and a small refrigerator.

"They're supposed to send up a playpen for Jonah." Riggs put the groceries away.

"Good thinking." She plugged in her cell phone and then turned to Kay-Kay. "Let's get you cleaned up first."

"Aw. A bath?" Kay-Kay whined.

"You have the most beautiful blond curly hair, so let's make it shine." Stormy smiled. "Besides, one of these days you might not mind so much." She grabbed the baby shampoo and headed into the bathroom. She ran a bath for Kay-Kay and washed her hair. The girl's long hair was tangled, but after a few minutes of scrubbing, Stormy had it soft and grime-free.

After Kay-Kay was dressed, Stormy reran a small amount of water for Jonah and gave him a quick bath. Once the baby was dressed in his new clothes from the backpack, she checked her phone.

The screen lit up, but the cracks kept her from being able to read it. She let out a breath.

"Does it work?" Riggs asked.

"Maybe. The screen is so messed-up, I can't read it. But it seemed to power up. I'll let it charge some more." She grabbed her new denim capris, a soft pink T-shirt and underclothes and headed for the bathroom. A plastic bag from the store sat on the bed, and she took it, too. "I'll be out in a few minutes."

"I'll order pizza, if that's okay with you."

Stormy glanced at Kay-Kay. "Do you like pizza?"

"Yeah!" Her smiled faded. "But Jonah only chews the crust. He'll choke if he takes a bite."

"You're a good big sister." Riggs rubbed her head. "We have special food for him."

After showering and dressing, she stepped into the cool room. The air conditioner blew cold, giving her chills. She wanted nothing more than to lie down and sleep for thirty minutes, but they had too many things to do. "Are you going to shower?"

Riggs sighed. "I need to. Won't take me two minutes."

True to his word, Stormy had just enough time to brush her hair and was halfway through using the blow-dryer when Riggs stepped out of the bathroom with his hair wet. The black T-shirt fit snug over his muscular build, and his jeans were relaxed fit.

He glanced up at her, and suddenly she blushed. What was she doing staring at him? She got busy putting her brush away and pretended to be busy.

"You might as well relax. We can go out after we eat."

She went back into the bathroom and finished blow-drying her hair. She applied mascara and light pink lipstick that she'd picked up from the store. The new white baseball cap felt fresh and so much better than the one she'd been wearing. She tossed it back into her bag—she could wash it later.

The pizza was there, along with canned soda. They took a seat on the edge of the bed, and Riggs put Jonah on his knee.

As they put slices on paper towels to prepare to eat, Riggs paused before he took a bite. "Is it all right if we say a blessing?"

"Certainly." She looked into his brown eyes and noticed the emotion.

He cleared his throat and offered a short thanks for the food. They ate in silence, the greasy pizza tasting better than it ought to. Riggs fed Jonah small bites, alternating between spoonfuls from jars of peas and peaches, in between eating his own pizza slice. *Ew.* Peas by themselves just didn't sound that appetizing, but no doubt that was healthier than their pizza. Stormy probably should've offered to take turns with him so Riggs could enjoy his meal, but he seemed content.

Riggs's eyes glistened as he fed the boy and watched Kay-Kay. Stormy found herself mesmerized by the man's expression. So tough and serious. The rancher didn't look like the doting type, but the softness in his gaze said otherwise.

By the time Stormy was through eating, so were the kids. "I'll take him so you can finish eating."

Riggs wiped his mouth with a paper towel. "No, I'm good. We need to get going."

"Are you certain? You only ate two slices."

"I can always eat more later if I get hungry, but I'm eager to check out that address."

Stormy said, "Yeah. I hope it's not all for nothing."

Kay-Kay flounced back on the bed. "Can we go swimming? I saw a pool."

"Maybe later." Stormy knew the kids had to be tired of traveling and were ready for some fun. "I know you'd love to play in the pool, but we have somewhere to go."

"Aw." Kay-Kay threw her hands back on the bed. "Okay. Can we get a toy?"

Riggs smiled. "We can make that happen."

"Yay! Thank you, Riggs." She scrambled from the bed and gave his legs a hug.

Stormy hoped they could stop after they were done checking out the address to get some toys for the children. The kids had been through so much the past day, and probably even longer. She didn't know how long they had been at that house. It wasn't too much to ask.

Treat Yourself with 2 Free Books!

Romance

Suspense

GET UP TO 4 FREE BOOKS & 2 FREE GIFTS WORTH OVER $20

See Inside For Details

Claim Them While You Can

Get ready to relax and indulge with your **FREE BOOKS** and more!

**Claim up to FOUR NEW BOOKS & TWO MYSTERY GIFTS –
absolutely FREE!**

Dear Reader,

We both know life can be difficult at times. That's why it's important to treat yourself so you can relax and recharge once in a while.

And I'd like to help you do this by sending you this amazing offer of up to FOUR brand new full length FREE BOOKS that WE pay for.

This is everything I have ready to send to you right now:

Try **Love Inspired® Romance Larger-Print** books and fall in love with inspirational romances that take you on an uplifting journey of faith, forgiveness and hope.

Try **Love Inspired® Suspense Larger-Print** books where courage and optimism unite in stories of faith and love in the face of danger.

Or **TRY BOTH!**

All we ask in return is that you answer 4 simple questions on the attached Treat Yourself survey. You'll get **Two Free Books** and **Two Mystery Gifts** from each series you try, *altogether worth over $20*! Who could pass up a deal like that?

Sincerely,

Pam Powers

Harlequin Reader Service

Treat Yourself to Free Books and Free Gifts.

Answer 4 fun questions and get rewarded.

We love to connect with our readers! Please tell us a little about you...

	YES	NO
1. I LOVE reading a good book.	○	○
2. I indulge and "treat" myself often.	○	○
3. I love getting FREE things.	○	○
4. Reading is one of my favorite activities.	○	○

TREAT YOURSELF • Pick your 2 Free Books...

Yes! Please send me my Free Books from each series I select and Free Mystery Gifts. I understand that I am under no obligation to buy anything, as explained on the back of this card.

Which do you prefer?

❑ **Love Inspired® Romance Larger-Print** 122/322 IDL GRDP
❑ **Love Inspired® Suspense Larger-Print** 107/307 IDL GRDP
❑ **Try Both** 122/322 & 107/307 IDL GRED

FIRST NAME	LAST NAME

ADDRESS

APT.#	CITY

STATE/PROV.	ZIP/POSTAL CODE

EMAIL ❑ Please check this box if you would like to receive newsletters and promotional emails from Harlequin Enterprises ULC and its affiliates. You can unsubscribe anytime.

LI/SLI-520-TY22

A few minutes later, they were in their rented truck and headed toward Amarillo. Stormy looked out the window at the wide-open spaces and the moderate traffic on the road. She didn't remember ever being here, but what did she really know about her past or where she'd been?

Was she happy, maybe pursuing a career of her dreams? Did she have a mom, dad, siblings or a boyfriend? As her mind kept returning to these thoughts, she was afraid she didn't want to know. Was she better off moving on with her life and not knowing her past?

Riggs glanced her way, and his face softened. His hand reached across the console and patted her hand. "Everything will be all right."

She appreciated the encouragement, but she wondered what she would do if it weren't. *Please, Lord, don't let me be the criminal I see in my dreams.*

Riggs listened as the GPS directed them to the address written on the note. According to his quick search before they'd left, the address belonged to a small vacation home, one of those that people rent for several days. He didn't like having Kay-Kay and Jonah with them in case everything went awry, but he simply didn't have a safe place to leave them.

If he had more time, he could've made a few phone calls to see if any of his family or friends could watch them. But Stormy was ready to find the holding house, not that he blamed her.

He turned left for a block and then a right. The small clapboard house sat neatly in the trees and had a sizable yard. A newer-model white sedan sat under the carport. He slowed but kept going.

"Wait. That was it." Stormy plastered her face against the window. "Go back."

"We need to check it out before we go barging up to the door." When he touched her hand this time, she flinched. He brought his hand back to his side of the cab. "Sorry."

She brought her hand to her chest.

Why did he do that? He shouldn't have touched her. Had no right. More than likely, her memory would come flooding back and she would be out of his life in a heartbeat. Probably had someone special in her life already. But she hadn't resisted when he kissed her earlier. *Don't do this, Riggs. You know better.* He wasn't ready for a relationship. Might never be ready.

At the end of the street, he turned the truck around and headed back. "Would you let me go to the door first?"

Her head jerked toward him. "Let me do it. You stay in the truck with kids."

A little voice came from the back seat. "Can I get out?"

She turned around. "I'm sorry, honey, but you need to stay inside for now."

"Come on, Stormy." Riggs cleared his throat. "These people won't know me, but they might recognize you. Until we know why that address was in your backpack, we need to play it safe. This is a vacation rental. As far as we know, you used the place in the past and whoever is there now is a stranger. Or maybe it's someone who is involved in a kidnapping ring, and they're just waiting for their opportunity to bring you down."

She opened her mouth as if to argue but then clamped it shut again. Drawing a deep breath, she said, "You're right. Go to the door and find out how many are there and who they are. I'll stay with kids."

"Thank you." Besides, he'd helped her off his ranch and had no right to demand anything of her. But if he'd still been an agent with the FBI, there was no way the discussion would've taken place. Riggs liked to think he'd mellowed since then. Memories of Macy Sue crossed his mind, her sweet smile. Identical to Kay-Kay's.

Stormy had no idea how badly he'd wanted to leave them at the hotel until he'd checked this out for himself. He'd do anything to keep them safe.

"I'll be right back."

She smiled apprehensively. "Don't take long."

After he climbed out of the truck, he glanced around. A dog barked somewhere. A few cars were parked on the street, but most sat in their driveways. This was a quiet neighborhood, and nothing looked out of place.

As he approached, he kept watch on the windows for movement, but saw none.

Before his finger touched the doorbell, the door swung open.

A tall, dark-haired lady stood in the door, one hand behind her back. "Who are you and what do you want?"

The feeling she held a weapon slapped him upside the head. For all his mental prepping, he hadn't planned for this. Was anyone else in the house?

TEN

Stormy leaned against the window, trying to get a better view. She'd seen the door open, but Riggs blocked her view of the person standing there.

Jonah jabbered from the back seat.

"I want out," Kay-Kay grumbled.

"Just a minute." Stormy didn't take her eyes from the house. For a few moments, Riggs didn't move. He must be talking to the person. As the seconds ticked by, she felt he must've been right about the person or people staying there having nothing to do with her. He and the person were probably talking about the cool tourist places to visit in the area.

She couldn't help but hope this was a good lead, but her heart sank a little.

Finally, Riggs turned around and strode back to her window. She opened the passenger door. "What is it?"

"Come on. This lady claims she knows you."

Stormy's heart pounded faster as she climbed out of the vehicle. "Who is she?"

Riggs went to the back door to let the kids and Shotgun out. "You'll see."

Why did people have to be so secretive? Was it that

serious or disappointing? He wouldn't be getting the kids out if it were dangerous, but by his serious expression, she didn't know what to expect.

Riggs carried Jonah and headed across the street with Shotgun at his side.

Kay-Kay skipped along beside them. "I wonder if they have toys."

Stormy mumbled, "I doubt it." Of course, she knew nothing about the person in the house, so why cast doubt to the girl?

As she stepped to the entrance, the wooden door opened behind the glass. A twenty something brunette with compassionate eyes looked her over.

The woman said, "Come on in, Stormy."

There was something familiar about her. The smile. The eyes. The dark curly hair. Stormy bluntly asked, "Who are you?"

Before she answered, the woman glanced down to Kay-Kay. "There are some toys in a tub in the living room."

Kay-Kay looked up with shining eyes. "Can I?"

Stormy was hesitant, for she always felt protective, but she relented. "Go ahead, just stay where I can see you."

"Okay." She made for the container of toys.

"I'm Josie Hunt." The woman laid her hand on Stormy's shoulder. "We work cases together."

Josie Hunt. The name did sound familiar. *Cases together.* "Are we with law enforcement?"

She shook her head. "I'm not exactly, but you are. But we both work alongside them. Do you remember anything?"

Stormy shrugged. "You look familiar, and your name is, too."

"We both work for the Bring the Children Home Project under Bliss Walker."

Memories started forming. "Bliss is an older, pretty woman."

Josie nodded. "Yes. She's the founder of our organization. We assist authorities in finding and bringing missing children home."

"Bliss had a child go missing." The memory shook Stormy. "A boy. He still hasn't been found."

"Right."

"You're an investigator…" Her world began to spin as the other team members came to mind. How could she forget something so important? "And I'm a weapons instructor for the police department?" Excitement built. Working for the police department couldn't be bad.

Riggs stood off to the side and out of the way.

Josie nodded and said, "You were here to check out a tip on two missing children, but you didn't report in. You should've called me two nights ago. What happened?"

Yes. It was a firm rule. You don't go off on your own. Always wait for backup. Constantly keep the team abreast of the situation. "I'm uncertain why I didn't call in. But that's Kay-Kay and Jonah."

Josie nodded. "The Ferrell kids. They went missing three weeks ago from their home in a suburb of Fort Worth."

The details swirling through her head cleared. Stormy added, "I remember now. They were taking a nap while their mom was doing laundry on the other end of the house. The washer and dryer were in a garage or something that made it difficult to hear. When the mom went to check on the kids later, their beds were empty."

"Yes." Josie smiled. "You do remember. Let's sit down. Would you like something to eat or drink?"

"No, thanks. We just ate." Stormy followed her to a small dining table just off the kitchen. The room had an open concept and connected to the kitchen and living room. Riggs put Jonah on the floor close to Kay-Kay before he sat on the hearth.

The more the memories returned, the more her heart swelled, and she listed them off. "I'm not married. I'm from Liberty, a small town north of Dallas. I went to school in Liberty—home of the Fighting Wildcats. My best friend was Kristina Kaufman." Her smile widened. "She was the only person who could beat me in the mile in junior high. We got caught in Lambert's barn pretending to smoke a pipe—we had no tobacco—that we had taken from the old man's secret location in the cab of a broken-down tractor. When we jumped out of the hayloft, Kristina hit a piece of tin on the way down, which earned her twelve stitches. My mom was not happy when—"

Josie smiled, but her expression was stilted, like she understood Stormy was working through her amnesia. "I didn't know you back in school."

Stormy's mom and dad. Suddenly, her mouth went dry. She tried to swallow but couldn't. Her family. Her mom. And her *dad*!

"What is it?" Josie asked.

Stormy mumbled, "I'm Annie Tillman."

Riggs turned toward her.

Josie said, "Yeah. Stormy Fowler is your undercover name. Are you all right?"

No, of course she wasn't all right. She was Annie Tillman. Her birth name Annie *Craddick*. She had gladly taken on her stepdad's name when her mother divorced her father and remarried.

She hadn't seen her dad in years, not since she was twelve. The night that changed her life forever.

Riggs got up and took the chair next to her. "What's wrong?"

She tried to force a smile. She'd been hiding from herself most of her life. Even her closest friends didn't know the truth.

And they weren't going to find out today.

For just a short time, amnesia had blessed her, and she had forgotten all about her dad. A whole day free of his crimes, like breaking a chain connected to a block of cement hanging around her neck as she tried to keep her head above water. "Nothing. Absolutely nothing." She turned her attention back to Josie. "Are you going to take these children back to their family?"

"I can." Intense brown eyes stared at her. "But you know the rules. You need to fill out the report so Bliss can turn them over to government agencies. We go through the authorities. Someone from social services must transport the children."

"Of course. I don't know what I was thinking." The returning memories hurled her into a whirlwind.

Josie got to her feet with her cell in her hand. "Speaking of Bliss, I need to call her and let her know that you're here and safe." She disappeared down a hall to the back part of the house.

Annie glanced at Riggs and noted his eyebrows had drawn together in concern. How silly she'd been. She had fallen for the cowboy. The man was honest. No wonder the way he cared for the children had touched her heart. She had never known such love. Riggs didn't know what kind of blood ran through her veins.

Memories of watching her father kidnap two terrified girls when she was twelve years old and shoving them into the van where Annie waited had changed the course of her life forever—the image permanently ingrained in her brain. What had she been thinking, getting close to a man? Her father was a monster. Kidnapping innocent children so he could sell them on the adoption black market. What kind of person did that? What kind of father could look his daughter in the eyes after he destroyed other kids' lives? Had she meant nothing to the man?

Deep down, the fear bubbled through her very being, hoping—praying—she hadn't inherited his evil. The fear festered in her heart that if she really considered it, she might be a terrible human—and parent. So she worked as hard and fast as she could to save as many children as possible, afraid to stop. Afraid to let her guard down. If she could find one more child, prevent one more abduction, teach one more mom or teen to protect herself, maybe—just maybe—it would be enough. But she knew it wouldn't.

Could she ever be free of her father's evil?

One thing she did know, as long as she lived—no matter the cost—she would continue to search for and help find missing children. She could never live with herself if she stopped. There was no time for vacation or to rest. If she relaxed, another child got taken.

"Are you okay?" Riggs's voice pulled through her thoughts.

For a moment, she simply stared at him. "I'm not like him."

"Who?" Confusion crossed his brow.

She shook her head, ignoring his question. "I'm going back for the rest of the kids. I know they're in that house."

His dark eyes took her in, seemingly trying to read her mind. "That's fine, Annie. I wouldn't expect you to forget about those kids. But I'm going to help you. I want you to stay safe, and we need to wait on your team."

She drew a deep breath and looked at the ceiling. "If we wait, the abductors will relocate the children." Her gaze turned back to him. "We must move fast."

As if he knew better than to argue, he nodded and covered her hand with his. The warmth penetrated her skin. "We will find these children."

She was glad he'd agreed, because no matter what, she intended to rescue them.

He got up and gave her shoulder a gentle squeeze. "You're a good person, Annie Tillman."

Tears pooled in her eyes, but she didn't reply for fear her voice would crack and give her emotional state away. He had no idea what his words meant to her. *Thank you.*

Riggs could tell the moment Annie become a block of ice—cold and detached. She ceased making eye contact, and her body become rigid.

What had she recalled? She'd claimed she wasn't married, so that wasn't it. Her back was straight and her shoulders back. It didn't surprise him she was a weapons instructor, ever since he'd witnessed her take down Waylon and handle herself coolly in the attack.

Her green eyes held a storm of emotions, much like her undercover name.

Josie returned the table and glanced at Annie, and then at him, making Riggs wonder what she was thinking. Did she sense the change in Annie's demeanor like him? Then she said, "Annie, tell me what you remember about the children's rescue."

"I'm afraid not much. It was a two-story red farmhouse with a front porch—not a wraparound. I don't remember the location or how to get there, but it was in the middle of nowhere. And if I recall right, a fair distance from the road."

"In the trees or in the open?"

Annie squinted as if trying to remember. "A few trees, but mainly in the open. And there were several vehicles parked outside."

Josie nodded. "That's good information. Can you describe them?"

She shrugged. "A minivan and three cars, I think."

"What about the takedown? How were you able to find Kay-Kay and Jonah?"

Annie frowned. "I don't know. I simply don't remember. I just have a vision of the house, not the people or how I found the children."

"Okay. That's good." Josie continued to nod calmly. "Were there other children at the home?"

"Yeah. I'm certain there were. I believe several. No names or faces, just a feeling."

"Okay, sounds like it may be a holding house. How did you learn the location? The last time you checked in, you were investigating a lead, and you promised to call if you learned anything."

Annie fidgeted with her hands. "I don't know. I can't remember that part, either. I recall how important it is not to go in by ourselves, but to always wait for backup from the team or law enforcement. It's one of the first rules." Her hand went to her head, like she had a headache. "I simply can't remember how I got the kids."

Concern for Annie surprised Riggs. He'd fallen fast for the woman, which was uncharacteristic for him. It had taken the summer months in between semesters for him to ask Claire out. Maybe he'd been alone too long. That was it. It was time he joined society again and quit staying on his ranch so much. Maybe he should call his brothers or mom and go in for a visit.

"We'll ensure Kay-Kay and Jonah are returned to their parents and then work with the local sheriff's department to see about locating the place."

Annie put on what he was certain was a forced smile in response.

Frustration bit at Riggs. He should be happy, but he wasn't. What if the guys hunting them made another attack? He cleared his throat. "I don't like it."

Both women looked at him like they'd forgotten he was in the room.

"What do you not like, Mr. Brenner?" Josie turned her brown eyes on him, her scrutiny too sharp for someone of her young age.

Jonah worked himself across the carpet to the television cord. Riggs got up and moved him back to the center of the room, to where Kay-Kay was pretending to feed her doll. Jonah's chubby hands clutched his shirt, but Riggs pulled him away and put him on the floor.

He turned to the women. "Those men meant to kill Stormy, uh, Annie—I like Annie better, by the way. The name fits you. Anyway, I realize we haven't filled you in, Josie, but it makes me wonder who's behind the attacks. No doubt it's people from the home where the children are being kept, but who are they? And what will they do to keep Annie quiet?"

Josie stared at him for a moment. "Who are you again?"

"Riggs Brenner."

The team member cocked her head. "A rancher?"

"Yes, ma'am."

Annie waved her hand. "He's good. I never could've made it without his help, but don't let that cowboy act fool you. He used to be an FBI agent."

"Hmm." Josie's gaze lingered on him before she addressed Annie. "Maybe you should go back over everything that has happened."

Riggs got up from the hearth and walked to the front of the house and glanced out the kitchen window while Annie went back over the attacks with Josie. Heat burned his cheeks. Why was he always hesitant to mention he used to be law enforcement? Because he was ashamed he hadn't made the cut, and because of his bad choices, he'd lost both his wife and daughter. Guilt ate at him. Other agents balanced careers and home life just fine. But he'd taken it too far.

He listened and continued to take in their surroundings. Besides his truck, no other vehicles sat on the street that weren't there before. He walked through the living room and glanced out to the backyard without moving the miniblinds.

A wooden fence divided their yard from the neighbors. Four lawn chairs surrounded a fire pit on the patio, and a tower play set complete with a slide and swings stood in the corner. Two large oak trees cast shade across most of the area, making it a comfortable vacation home. If it were him renting the house, he would've preferred a little more acreage for privacy, but he supposed it beat staying in a hotel.

Nothing suspicious caught his attention.

He continued to listen as Annie wrapped up her report to Josie. Hearing the events again convinced him the danger would not subside until the men were caught or Annie was dead.

Should he call Agent Clayton McCarthy, his former FBI partner, and fill him in? Maybe just a heads-up? He wasn't trying to involve himself more in the case or take over the Bring the Children Home team, but what if this was bigger than they realized?

Clayton and a couple of other agents had worked on missing children's cases in his department. They tried to find not only the children but also the people at the top of kidnapping or trafficking rings.

Yes. Even though it'd be three years since he'd touched base with his old friend, he'd call Clayton. It couldn't hurt to have more people working on the case.

"Riggs." Annie's voice had him turning. Her green eyes connected with his, and his chest tightened, making it difficult to catch his breath.

"I can get the rest of my stuff at the hotel in Josie's car while she watches the kids."

No. Hadn't she been listening? This was dangerous.

Annie said, "I can do this without you."

Claire's last words to him. The last time he'd seen her. Like a sucker punch to his gut, the pain as raw and deep as it was that day when he put off their anniversary plans. *You're free to stay. We'll make it without you.*

He wouldn't make the same mistake twice.

ELEVEN

Annie remained at the table after Riggs strode off to the living room to be with the kids. She could tell by his stony expression and the twitch in his jaw he wasn't happy with her. Annie had been thinking it was time to bury herself in her work again. That's how she coped with being a criminal's offspring. Lower her head and push full steam ahead, forgetting everything but her mission.

Josie returned to the table after leaving a message for their boss.

If only Annie could remember what leads she was following, she might easily find the farmhouse again. "I need to know more about the case. What exactly led me to West Texas?"

Josie stared at her for a second. "You were frustrated."

That didn't sound good. "Why is that?"

"Because—"

"Because I had called you two other times about the vehicle." Annie completed the thought as the memories kept tumbling back. She sighed. "I remember now. I was trying to track down the car someone had seen near the Ferrell home around the time of the abduction." At Josie's nod, she continued. "And you found the vehicle on a surveillance camera from the neighborhood bank but only a few digits of the license plate could be seen."

"Right."

"Okay. That sounds like a good place to start. I'll pick back up where I left off."

"Annie, be careful and don't go running into a hornet's nest without backup. I know you want to solve this case, just like each one you work." Josie's brown eyes studied her. "I've never told you this, but you're one of the best officers we have on the team. Your dedication is off the charts. It's always impressed me how you'll stay at homeless shelters or integrate with people you see most likely to become victims."

Annie swallowed. She wasn't used to hearing compliments.

Her friend cleared her throat. "But I must warn you. Sometimes you take it too seriously. You give up everything in your life to help people, and while that's commendable, sometimes you put yourself in danger. And everyone needs balance—joy." She glanced toward Riggs, who sat on the floor beside the kids, and then Josie refocused on her. Her voice lowered to a whisper. "He seems like a good man."

Annie straightened and lowered her voice as well. "I know you mean well, but besides him helping me at his ranch, Riggs has nothing to do with me. You're reading too much into this." She tried to keep the annoyance out of her tone but was afraid she'd failed. How could she explain that she and Riggs couldn't be anything more than friends? Annie didn't know what kind of mom she'd be. If she married, surely the person would want kids, and she would keep no man from the wonders of children. What if Annie failed to develop an attachment to her kids, like her father? What if she turned out just like him? She couldn't take the chance.

Josie continued to scrutinize her, evidently not convinced of her proclamation. "Riggs said you had to go to the hospital. Did the doctor comment on the cause of your amnesia?"

Annie sighed. "She didn't think the bump on my head was severe enough to cause that much damage, but emotional trauma may've triggered the condition."

Josie didn't respond but stared at her with concern.

She tapped her foot on the floor, as she was ready to move on to another conversation. "Back to my research."

Her friend reached across the table and took her hand, then quickly released it. "Sorry. I forgot how you don't like that touchy-feely stuff."

She couldn't resist a glance at Riggs to see if he'd overheard, and awkwardness filled her, as he was staring too hard at the carpet too long. *Great, just great.*

Was she really that cold? She didn't mean to be. Just wanted to keep her distance. She couldn't hurt people if she kept her distance, right? "The first person I checked out with a similar license plate wound up being a dead end."

"Both people you checked out," Josie said "First the elderly man in the assisted living facility whose car hadn't been driven in over a year."

Annie nodded, recalling the detail. "And the second was the owner who had wrecked his car in the months previous. The vehicle's new home is a junkyard."

"Right. It's all coming back to you."

Not that it helped. Failure surrounded her. She'd wanted this case since it first came across her desk. As a trainer at the police academy, her lieutenant set her hours at eight to five every day, and every three months she had a week off. She used the extra time to work missing children's cases. Many nights and weekends were also spent working cases or offering training in self-defense classes, especially to women and children. Anything to help people fight against wouldbe abductors.

"The Ferrell case was taking too long." If Annie kept thinking out loud, maybe everything would become clearer. "It's common knowledge the first few days of an abduction are key to finding the missing. First, there weren't many clues in the case. Even though the children had been taken in broad daylight, most people were busy with their business and didn't notice the car in front of the modest home. The mother hadn't seen or heard anything, which made investigators believe there was more than one kidnapper. A back window had been found open in the nursery."

Josie nodded. "Right. I have the files if you'd like to look them over again."

"Thanks. I'd like that. Can I have a hard copy? All my information is in my missing Jeep."

"No problem. I can get that for you right now." Josie stood. "Seems like it won't be long and you'll be back to normal." Her coworker disappeared into a hallway leading to the back of the house.

"Yeah." *Normal.* Annie wasn't certain she liked the sound of that. But Josie was right. She could step right back into her old life of weapons training and selfdefense classes, all the while trying to bring missing children home. But why did she feel like something was missing?

She glanced to the living room.

Riggs scooped Jonah up from the floor, and immediately the baby put his fingers in Riggs's mouth. The cowboy playfully pretended to chew on his fingers, making a smile light up Jonah's face. The boy's glistening eyes displayed trust and love at the man.

Kay-Kay scrambled to her feet with the doll. "Look, Riggs, the baby is crying."

He took the baby in his free hand and pretended to look it over. "Looks hungry to me. Have you tried feeding her?"

The four-year-old smiled and snatched the doll back. "No, but I will." Kay-Kay cradled the doll and gazed into the plastic face. "I'm going to get you a bottle. Okay?"

Like Josie said, maybe Annie was missing balance.

Putting off the inevitable would benefit no one. Since the kids felt comfortable with Josie, Annie would tell Riggs he could return to his ranch today, and she no longer needed his help.

She did her best to ignore Riggs playing with the kids. The tension in the room was obvious, and she didn't want to hurt him, but it was best this way.

He looked at the kids and then back at her. "I don't like it. There's been too many attacks. Let me take you back to the hotel to get your things while Josie watches the kids."

The more time she spent with him, the harder it was going to be. She liked him, an easy thing to admit. Not only was he handsome, but the way Riggs tended to the kids—she would've done anything to have a father care for her like Riggs had for the two children. His nurturing said a lot about the man. The gunmen had blown up his house. Many people, probably herself included, would've dwelled on the loss, but not him.

How had Riggs put aside the destruction while he continued to help?

Inhaling a deep breath, she finally said, "Fine. You're probably right. Take me back to the hotel. We'll get our things and then you can drop me off."

He nodded. "Let's go."

She walked over to the kids. "Kay-Kay, Riggs and I are going to leave for a little while, but we'll be back. Are you okay here with Josie?"

Kay-Kay looked up at her and frowned. "Don't leave me." She ran to Riggs and held out her arms. "Hold me. Hold me."

Riggs glanced at Stormy. He knelt beside the girl and wrapped his arms around her. "We'll be back."

Annie had wanted to wait to tell Kay-Kay that she was going home, but seeing the girl was scared to be left again, she reconsidered. "We're working to get you and Jonah home to your mom and dad."

"Mommy and Daddy?" Her eyes grew big. "Yes! Can we go now?"

"Not yet, Kay-Kay bug." Riggs scrubbed her head. "Tomorrow. We're going to the hotel to pick up our things, but you can stay with Josie to play with the toys."

Her face fell. "Okay. Can Shotgun stay with us?"

"Sure. But take good care of him."

"I will." She nodded happily.

Annie watched Riggs pick up Jonah and give him a kiss on top of his head. The man mumbled something to the baby that sounded suspiciously like "love" before putting him back on the floor. She gave both children a kiss on the cheek goodbye.

Josie returned with the case files, handed them to Annie, and followed them to the door. With her hand on the knob, she said, "I'll update Bliss on what's going on."

Josie was right. Bliss took every case personally. Annie expected to find the children but also wanted her team to remain safe. "I appreciate that."

"Do you have your phone?"

"Hopefully, I can stop by the phone store to see if it's repairable. If not, I'll buy a new one."

"Okay, let me know." Josie gave her a funny look.

"What was that look for?"

"Nothing. I've just never seen you this way."

Annie laughed. "I don't know what you're talking about."

"Whatever you say," Josie said, smiling. "Y'all be careful."

Annie called over her shoulder to the kids, "We'll be right back."

She and Riggs got in the truck and headed to the hotel. After a few minutes, the silence grew awkward. There were so many things she wanted to say but couldn't, even though Riggs deserved the truth.

Riggs grabbed her hand. "Promise me you'll be careful and let me know when the kids make it back to their family."

"I will." She shot him a smile. "I can't thank you enough for your help with the kids."

He merely nodded. For the third time, his gaze went to the rearview mirror. "I must say it again. I don't like the attacks. There's nothing to say the men won't strike again. I don't like you and Josie being alone with Kay-Kay and Jonah. If the men are still after you, it could put all of you in danger."

"I keep thinking about that, too."

"You could leave the Amarillo area and come back later."

Her head jerked. "I must find the holding house and save those kids. Leaving is not an option."

As they pulled into the hotel parking lot, a group of teenagers piled into a church van. She was glad they were leaving the hotel. Too many potential victims in case the men found their location.

As if Riggs's thoughts were in line with hers, he said, "I've decided to call my brother and stay with him. I can't put innocent people in danger. You're welcome to go with me."

"No, thanks." She answered without thinking, but the thought of putting others in the line of fire was out of the question for her, too. Still, she needed to go on her own way.

It didn't take five minutes to gather their things from the hotel. When she was seated back in the passenger side of the truck, she checked her phone again. She still couldn't read it. "Can we stop by a phone place and buy me a replacement? I'm hoping they can transfer my information to a new one."

"Sure."

Guilt at how easily Riggs wanted to help weighed on her. "Never mind. You've done too much for me already. I can go to the store later."

"I don't mind. Have you remembered where your vehicle is or how you got into the canyon?"

"No, I don't know where my Jeep is. I have so much

to do. I probably should call the insurance company, but I don't even know if my Jeep is drivable. Why can't I remember rescuing the kids or what took place?"

"I don't know." He shrugged. "Sometimes trauma brings on amnesia. Kind of like someone in a car accident, you may never recall the minutes leading to or following the wreck. I need to call my insurance company, too. I'll do that from my brother's if I can reach them before closing time."

"Where will you stay long term?"

"After this case is over, and I'm certain the danger is in the past, I suppose at a hotel."

Inwardly, she sighed. She hated this. "Don't you have anyone who can put you up for a few nights?"

"My brother wouldn't mind, but I hate to put him and his family out long term. He has a wife and two daughters. Besides, I'd like to be closer to my ranch, so the drive isn't long. My brother's family and my mom are on the west side of Amarillo. My family is close-knit. I have a friend who owns a large RV that I'm sure he'd let me use. Or I could just buy my own. It will take a while to rebuild if I decide to."

Annie laid her head back on the headrest and closed her eyes. So much had happened, but at least her memory had all but returned, except for the details of rescuing the kids.

The vision of the house returned. A large red house. White shutters. She could see the vehicles that sat in the drive. A black Suburban. Two cars, a silver sedan and a pearl-blue convertible with a white soft top. She remembered the sports car because it had white leather seats—something she'd always loved. That car had been expensive. A truck sat under the cover of a willow tree. She tried to bring it all into focus. Red or maroon, maybe? That was it. She guessed it was the same maroon truck as the one Waylon drove in the canyon.

"Did you remember something else?"

Annie opened her eyes and looked at him. "I was just thinking about the house where the kids were kept."

"Recall anything of value?" He shrugged. "I've lived in the area for several years. Maybe I could help pinpoint it."

"No additional details about the home, but the cars that sat out front."

"Care to share?"

Annie relayed what she remembered.

"A blue convertible. I would guess there weren't a lot of those in the canyon except from the occasional visitor. My ranch is too far off east and off the beaten path for most tourists visiting Palo Duro State Park to travel by. In my area, most people drive trucks or SUVs."

"I've noticed. Maybe that's why it stuck out to me." Suddenly, the sounds of kids yelling played through her mind. Two or more were fighting, and then a woman's voice admonished them to keep their voices down. Warned them the boss didn't like commotions. But that still didn't tell her where the house was located.

"Do you have a sense of where the house is?"

"I feel like it's south of the canyon, but I can't tell you why."

"Not *in* the canyon?"

"I don't think so. Or at least the image I have of the house was on flat land. Why can't I remember? The property had to be close for us to wind up on your ranch."

"Unless you drove a long way before your Jeep was disabled."

"Good point. I hadn't thought of that." But she still believed it was close. She looked at him, disappointed they wouldn't be working together. Suddenly, a funny feeling came over her. "You're not going to look for the holding house, are you?"

He stared out the driver's side window and then turned left. "I don't think so."

"Oh, come on. You are, aren't you?"

"I might drive around a bit. I need to make sure my horses are back at the barn and have plenty to eat first. Also need to check on my cattle. With the men entering my ranch, there's a good probability they didn't close the gate." He smiled sourly. "But you got me interested. If there are more kids out there, they need to be found."

She scrutinized him. "You want to find them before I get back? It's too dangerous! You're a capable man and all, but these men are killers. Besides, I'm sure if I drove the back roads, I could remember the location."

"I'm not stupid, Annie."

"Quit calling me Annie. Call me Stormy."

"Annie Tillman's your name."

But Tillman was her stepfather's name, not her dad's. It was when Josie mentioned Annie's name that she remembered who she was. *Really* was.

Nelson Craddick was her biological dad—a normal-appearing man on the outside who blended into society, but inwardly a money-hungry fiend who would stoop to any level to feed his insatiable selfish appetite. After her mom left her dad and married Steve Tillman, Annie had gladly moved to Steve's home in a town sixty miles away and taken on the name Tillman.

Nelson had taken the two girls from a homeless shelter when Annie was on a weekend visit with him. For years, Annie wondered why he'd abducted the kids while she was in the van. Why not wait until he was alone? Was he hoping to train her to be his accomplice? The thought made her sick. Later she learned he was under a self-imposed quota to provide four kids per month to the ringleader—identity still unknown. Not only was her father guilty of kidnapping, but also money laundering and counterfeiting. She remembered being at a sleepover at a friend's house and watching television when a crime program came on featuring her dad. The other girls didn't realize he was Annie's father. She called her mom to pick her up, and then she went home and cried all night.

Hurt and frustrated, she had gotten mad, thus claiming Stormy as her undercover name. Even her friends and her boss, Bliss Walker, didn't know her true identity. No matter how long she lived, no matter how many children she helped save, she could never escape from being Nelson Craddick's daughter.

Her father kidnapped and sold children. He climbed the criminal ladder of success, and it had landed him on the FBI's Most Wanted list.

Ever since she was twelve and witnessed her father abduct two girls from a homeless shelter by shoving them into the van while Annie watched in horror, she'd been running from herself.

Her mom had put the past behind her, or so it seemed. She'd married Steve, a general manager of a local grocery store and a good, God-fearing man. Mom seemed to enjoy being a stepmom to Steve's three children, ranging in age from twelve to twenty-two. When the kidnapping had first happened, her mom had listened to the story and offered comfort, but something told Annie that her mom never quite believed her. Her mom had never accused her of making the story up, but rather that Annie had misunderstood. How did someone misunderstand a kidnapping? Her mom had never suggested Annie receive counseling for the incident. Looking back, she realized that refusing to see what was in front of her was how her mom handled the betrayal of her husband. Shove it to the back of her mind and move on. Don't talk about it and pretend it never happened.

Denial of the facts seemed to work for her mother.

But Annie couldn't get the girls out of her mind and decided to make up for the harm her father had caused.

No matter how hard she worked, Annie couldn't teach enough women and children to protect themselves from the dangers. The list of victims kept growing and would continue to do so until someone brought the people at the top to justice.

If she could only do her part by finding and bringing down her father.

Once Kay-Kay and Jonah's case was over, she'd once again search for her father's trail. Which meant if she had to work with Riggs to rescue the children, so be it. The quicker, the better.

Annie said, "That's it. I'm staying here and going with you to look for the house. Josie has the children handled, even if it takes a day or two, and I'll try to be back in Fort Worth as soon as possible to see the kids."

His dark eyes turned to her, a question lingering like he was trying to read her. "Are you certain? I don't mind going it alone. I'm sure you're ready to get back to your old life."

"Riggs Brenner, I know what I want. I want to find that house with the kids. If I found the house once, I can do it again." He wasn't about to sway her from doing what was in her heart.

TWELVE

Anticipation filled Riggs now that Annie knew her identity. He prayed it didn't take long for her to find the holding house and for the people behind the abductions to be arrested. But worry also brimmed to the top of his mind. He hadn't been away from the FBI long enough to forget how a simple case could turn into a deadly, complicated wreck.

He'd finally gotten Annie to agree not to go back to Josie's rental house for fear it'd lead the assailants back to Kay-Kay and Jonah. She'd stick with him.

When they stopped for gas, Riggs rolled down his driver's window, put the nozzle in and called his brother. Annie had gone in to use the restroom but was now back in her seat.

"Hey, little brother, what's up?"

"I need a place to stay tonight. Well, actually, there's two of us. I have a friend with me." Even though Riggs didn't look at Annie, he could feel her eyes on him.

Gabe didn't hesitate. "Of course. You don't need to ask." His voice grew more serious. "Is anything wrong?"

An older-model Chevrolet truck pulled up to the

pump behind Riggs's truck. The man didn't look familiar, but Riggs didn't like talking in the open like this. "Ten-four. I'll explain it to you at the house, if that's all right."

"Affirmative. Catch you later when I get off work. You know where the key is if you get there first?"

"I remember how to get in. Thanks, Gabe." He clicked off, returned the nozzle to the pump and climbed in.

"He doesn't mind?" Annie asked.

"Naw. Gabe's a good guy. You'll like him and his family."

After they left the gas station, Riggs stopped by the phone store and had them check out Annie's phone. All her information had been lost, and since her device was damaged, she bought an inexpensive refurbished smartphone. Annie called Josie and asked to speak with Kay-Kay, because they had told the girl they would see her soon. Annie explained they wouldn't be coming back today.

Kay-Kay was busy playing with the toys and didn't seem concerned about them not stopping back by.

As they headed out of town to his brother's house, Riggs couldn't help but notice Annie stared out the window, silent. He would've thought she would be relieved things were moving in the right direction.

"What are you thinking?"

She turned to him. "Since I found the holding house, what led me there and why didn't I let my team members know? The car Josie and I were talking about must have led me to the house."

"Maybe you didn't know you were close to finding

the house. Maybe you wanted to check the house out and then you noticed the children."

"Could be," she said and rubbed her head. "I wish I could remember."

"I should've asked Gabe to search for all the property owners in the area for me. But I can do that when we get to his house."

"That's a good idea. Of course, someone could be renting the place, so the owner might not be aware of what is going on."

Riggs's cell phone lit up, and he recognized the sheriff's number. He held up his finger to Annie. "The sheriff."

At her nod, he answered the call. "This is Brenner."

"Sheriff Ludlam. I've been looking over the files, and I haven't found any credible leads, but I set aside all missing-children case files. I'm afraid most are runaways that don't want to be found. That happens a lot. And then we're supposed to find them, only for them to run away again. You're welcome to come by and look them over."

"I may do that." Riggs wondered if the sheriff was being completely honest or was being defensive of his office. Even though it was common for kids to run away for various reasons, that didn't mean some didn't want to be found. But there'd be no benefit to argue, since he'd offered access to the cases.

The sheriff continued, "I'm also sending my deputy and an investigator out to look at your house and any other evidence of the crime. I'd like for you to be there. Say about ten in the morning?"

Riggs was already planning to go by his ranch to check on Honey and Jack and his cattle, so he agreed.

When he disconnected, he filled Annie in on the conversation.

"I want to go find my Jeep in the morning."

"We will first thing." Riggs checked his rearview mirror again. A black Suburban followed about a block back and was slowly gaining on them. The driver might've been in a hurry, but Riggs pressed on the accelerator anyway. Driving on the outskirts of town, the speed limit was fifty-five, but being that it was after seven o'clock in the evening, the traffic was moderately heavy.

"What is it?" Annie turned around and looked out the back window. "Is that guy following us?"

"I'm not certain. Hang on. We're about to find out." He sped up to sixty-five, and the Suburban continued to gain. Up ahead, the highway came to an intersection. The SUV continued until he was on Riggs's bumper.

When Riggs arrived at the junction, he braked at the last minute and took a quick right, his tires squealing.

"Watch out!"

A sedan sat at the red light, and Riggs yanked hard to keep from swinging too far out, barely missing the back end of the car.

Another glance in his rearview mirror showed the SUV fly past the turn.

Riggs floored it, hoping to increase the distance. His brother lived on the southwest side of town, so he'd have to circle around after he lost this guy. At the next intersection, he took a left onto a less busy highway, hoping to get out of heavy traffic so they didn't endanger innocent people.

"I don't see him." Annie continued to look over her shoulder.

"If we can make it Gabe's, we should be all right."

"Didn't you say he had kids?" Wrinkles etched her forehead. "Do we really need to bring danger to their door?"

Riggs had wondered the same thing. "Gabe set his ranch up like a fortress. If I can lose these guys, and they don't find my brother's place, his family should be safe."

As Riggs cruised down the paved road, he came to a slow-moving minivan. He pulled in behind and, for the next couple of miles, followed it.

"I think we lost them. They probably thought we were continuing on the main highway."

"Could be." The words were no more out of his mouth than the black SUV topped the hill in front of them. Another rocky road appeared to his right, and he took it.

Annie gripped the handle as they spun through the bend. "I spoke too soon."

The SUV made the turn and bore down on them. A neon-green VW Bug convertible lumbered along in front of them.

Pop. Pop. Pop.

"Get down."

Instead of doing what he asked, Annie retrieved her gun from her backpack and prepared to return fire.

"There're teenagers in front of us," he yelled. "We've got to get off this road."

Annie rolled down her passenger window and took two shots. The SUV swerved but kept coming.

"Hold up. Railroad tracks ahead." But instead of going over them, Riggs jerked his wheel left, down the service road beside the tracks.

The SUV driver fired several more shots that went wild, the bumpy road making it difficult to aim.

A red dust cloud rose behind them. Riggs wasn't certain, but he thought the tracks lead to the small town of Little Beaver—population of fewer than two hundred people—and a lengthy bridge stood between them.

Keeping the pedal down, his speed climbed higher. Much too fast for this sandy road, but the driver of the SUV must have had a death wish, for he continued to gain.

Wuuuuunk! Wuuuuuuunk!

"Train!" Annie pointed in front of them. She put her seat belt back on.

The tracks were on the right side of the service road, and the bridge was just ahead. He kept his truck to the left side of the road, forcing the SUV to the right.

"Riggs! The road ends. There's…there's a bridge ahead."

"I know!" The Suburban sucked in behind them, its front bumper even with the back of his truck.

"That guy's going to kill us all!"

Not if Riggs could help it. There was a road in the field to the left that ran along the river.

Wuuuuuuunk! The forlorn warning sent chills down Riggs's spine as the engineer laid on the horn.

Bam. The SUV hit the back end of the truck, trying to force them off the road. Prepared for the move, Riggs kept control of the wheel. When the Suburban slowed, so did Riggs, not about to let them get into the inside lane so he could force Riggs's truck toward the train.

Pushing and shoving each other, the two vehicles fought for power, but the SUV's right wheels rode up on the tracks.

The train's brakes locked up, followed by hissing and screeching.

Annie grabbed her gun again, but Riggs put his hand out. "No. Stay down this time."

As they raced toward the bridge, the locomotive came straight for them, blowing the whistle and steam from the brakes rising. But a two-hundred-ton machine didn't have time to stop.

"Riggs!" She gripped the dash and prepared to crash.

The blasting horn and crunching gravel melted into one booming sound.

Just as the train was a mere twenty yards away, the driver in the SUV jerked his wheel and flew over the train tracks and to the other side.

The locomotive whizzed by, causing the ground to shake.

Riggs slammed on his brakes. The front end dipped down, and his truck rocked to a stop in the tall weeds, inches from going over the edge into the river. He backed up and came to a stop.

The train continued to whizz by, and a minute later, the caboose passed. Annie pointed. "The Suburban went over the side."

Riggs threw open the door and ran across the tracks, and Annie joined him.

The black SUV had left deep ruts down the steep incline and landed nose down in the shallow river. Two men struggled to get out.

"Come on," he said and nodded toward his vehicle. They both hurried to get in, and Riggs turned the truck around and headed back toward the road.

They both looked at each other.

Annie's face paled, and her hand went to her chest. "That was way too close."

He let out a deep breath. "I agree. Let's get to my brother's house before it gets dark and we have any more excitement for the day."

"I'm glad the kids weren't with us. Riggs, we need to find out who these guys are."

"We will. I intend to make some phone calls. We need more people helping us."

Riggs carried their things into the house after he'd introduced Annie to his brother.

Gabe pointed to the back bedroom. "Annie, you can put your things in the guest room. Second door on the left."

"I hate to put you out." Riggs held his suitcase and still considered staying at some other place. He didn't want to bring trouble to his brother and his family.

Gabe waved his hand through the air. "Nonsense. We don't mind."

"I really appreciate this. Where do you want me?" Riggs asked.

"Selena will probably put you in the office."

"Thanks." Riggs strode to the front of the house and put his things away. He'd known his brother would help them. When he returned to the living room, Gabe was sitting on the leather couch with a baseball game on but the volume turned down low.

"There's some soda in the refrigerator if you want one."

"Thanks. I may do that." He glanced at Annie as she whisked into the room. "You want one?"

"Yeah, sounds good. I'm thirsty."

After he gave her the can, Gabe joined them in the kitchen and took out a bag of chips and some dip. "I have nothing sweet, but if you're hungry for a snack, here you go."

Riggs opened the bag and dipped a wavy chip into the container. Annie did the same.

"I'm going to need to go on a diet later." Annie patted her stomach.

Gabe asked, "Would you prefer some grapes and cheese?"

"Do you mind? We had pizza earlier in the day."

"Not at all." His brother put the bunch of grapes in a bowl and laid cheddar cheese on a wooden chopping block with a knife and set them on the table. Gabe took a chair and joined them. "You want to talk about it?"

Riggs glanced at his brother's dark, concerned eyes. Gabe wouldn't pry, but his sibling cared. "I don't want to bring trouble to your door. We just need a place to hole up for the night. I'm going to meet investigators at the ranch in the morning."

"We have guns for protection."

"Not enough to fight off this gang, Gabe. They have assault rifles, and I have a feeling there's big money behind the group."

"A group? As in organized crime? You've got to be kidding me."

Riggs shook his head. "I wish I were. That's why I didn't come to family sooner."

"You're always welcome here, brother."

Riggs caught Gabe up on everything that had happened.

When he was through, Gabe looked at Annie. "So, you had amnesia? That must be wild."

She nodded. "Yeah, wild. It's not as glamourous as in the shows I've seen on television. Tends to make you doubt your sanity, and anyone could make up something about your past. You just pray your memory returns."

Gabe shook his head. "No, that doesn't sound like fun at all. And you hope there's not a prankster in the family." He smiled.

"Ah, cut it out, Gabe." Riggs sighed. "That sounds just like Brantley."

Annie looked from Gabe to Riggs. "Who's Brantley?"

Gabe grinned. "The oldest brother. He's a couple of years older than me."

"How's the rest of the family?" Guilt rode heavily on Riggs's shoulders. He'd been hiding for four years and avoided the reach outs. Right after Claire and Macy Sue's deaths, they'd called him often. After he continued to brush them off, they started calling him only on holidays the past couple of years.

"Good. Everyone misses you." Gabe glanced at Annie and then back to him. "Everyone understands you need time alone after Claire and Macy Sue were killed, but you ought to go see Mom. She worries about you. Always telling me and Brantley to go check on you. We keep reminding her you do everything in your own time."

Riggs noticed Annie took particular interest in the grape she held in her fingers. It was embarrassing to be reminded of the way he'd stepped away from his family. And he hadn't confided in her, either, about any of them. He should've at least mentioned what happened to his wife and daughter. Then Annie wouldn't have to hear it for the first time in front of his brother. "You're right. I'll go see Mom when all this is over."

"She'd appreciate that."

When Annie reached for the last slice of cheese, their eyes collided. Awkwardness hung between them, and he broke contact. What was she thinking? That he was a terrible brother and son for not visiting his family? Probably. Or maybe she just wondered why he hadn't mentioned his wife and daughter since they'd spent so much time together and he'd had plenty of opportunities.

Why hadn't he? Maybe he'd thought she'd judge him harshly. But it was time to move on and ask some of the questions he wanted answers to. "What do you know about Sheriff Rafe Ludlum?"

Gabe's eyebrow quirked. "The sheriff? Nothing, really. He's not in my county. I remember him running for office a few years back because his ads were everywhere. What was it? 'Stay safe with Rafe.'"

Annie choked on her drink. "You're kidding me. And he still won?"

Riggs smiled. "Yeah. Amazing, huh?"

"Something bothering you about the man?" Gabe took a swallow of his soda.

Gabe worked downtown for a large consulting company and was high up in the financial office. Not the CFO but working directly under him. His brother was an intelligent man, but also down-to-earth. He ranched on the side and helped coach his two daughters' Little League games. Gabe and Selena had a vast garden and sold produce at the farmers market. Kind of one of those perfect family types. Riggs was sure Gabe and

Selena had their share of arguments and problems, but he'd never know it. They seemed happy.

A tinge of jealously passed through Riggs. For just once, he wished he could be happy like that again. Even with all blessings his brother enjoyed, Gabe was easy to talk to and wasn't judgmental.

"I don't know. I guess Sheriff Ludlam could've just been doing his job." Riggs rubbed the back of his neck, the constant stress making his muscles tight and sore. "There was just something that turned me off. Made my antenna go up."

"You've always had a good sense about people, little brother. Is it you don't think he'll take you seriously, or that he can't be trusted?"

"I got the feeling he didn't want me and Annie looking into the missing children."

"That's not good." Gabe let out a low whistle. "Are you saying he's protective over his territory and wants you to let him handle it?"

"Maybe. It's not uncommon."

The back door opened, and Selena and his two nieces filed in.

"Riggs! How good to see you! I was wondering whose truck was parked out back." His sister-in-law's gaze went to Annie before coming back to him.

He got to his feet, and his two nieces hurried over to him. "Uncle Riggs," they said in unison. He gave all three of them a hug.

Selena's smile lingered a little longer, a mischievous gleam in her eye.

Riggs cleared his throat. "Selena, this is my friend Annie."

The women greeted one another with a smile and a quick handshake.

His sister-in-law patted her girls on the shoulder. "You two go get ready for bed and toss your dirty clothes outside your door. I'll get them washed before tomorrow's game."

Gabe looked at his wife. "Honey, Riggs and Annie are going to stay the night with us."

"That's wonderful." Her gaze went to the chips. "Oh, let me get you something more nutritious to eat."

Riggs held up his hand. "No, we're good. We had grapes and cheese. This was perfect."

"Has Gabe shown you the guest room?" Selena addressed Annie. At Annie's nod, Selena continued, "Come on, let me show you where everything is. You'll have your own bathroom. Give me time to pick things up."

Annie waved her hand. "I'm going to turn in. Good night."

Riggs stared after her.

Gabe's eyes met his, and he waited until his wife and girls had disappeared down the hall. "Have you called the judge?"

He referred to Judge Chadwick Jacobs, an old friend of their dad's. Over the years, when they had a legal question, they always went to Chad. Riggs remembered it was a call to Chad—at that time, a lawyer—that got the FBI brought in on his dad's murder case.

Their dad had gone to Amarillo to buy parts for a tractor and never returned home. Brantley, being the only son with a driver's license, drove into town and found their dad's truck parked at a gas station. There was no sign of their dad, though. A call to Chad, and within twenty-four hours, the FBI was on the case. They found their dad's body at an abandoned home just ten miles from his truck. Within the week, the FBI had arrested the perpetrator, and later, they prosecuted him for murder. His father, killed for a mere forty-three dollars he had in his pocket. McCarthy had been the agent on his dad's case who convinced Riggs to join the bureau, and later became his partner. "No, I haven't had time. Although it had crossed my mind. We need help."

Gabe got to his feet. "Jacobs is a good man and can always get something done. He'll also let you know if Ludlam has given him any problems."

"You're right." Riggs got up. "It couldn't hurt to talk to him."

"It's late. I'm going to bed. Let me know if you need anything."

"I will. And thanks, Gabe."

It was almost ten o'clock. As much as Riggs would've liked to visit with the judge tonight, he decided it was too late to call and resolved to talk to him in the morning.

He made a bed on the couch in the office. Annie was staying in the guest bedroom on the opposite end of the house, close to the girls' rooms. Gabe and Selena's suite was positioned on the back side of the house near the kids' rooms. The large bay window in the office overlooked the front yard. He closed the wooden blinds and turned off the light. A quick glance outside showed no movement, not that he expected anyone to be out there.

The ranch had an automatic gate complete with a camera and then a driveway a quarter of a mile long. A pipe fence surrounded the area by the county road, making it extra difficult to get to the house without driving through the neighbor's pasture along the back of the property.

Everyone had already turned in for the night, and he hadn't heard voices or footsteps for well over thirty minutes. Not able to relax, he quietly exited his room and walked through the dark house, only lit by the moonlight filtering through the windows. He was careful to be quiet so as not to wake anyone.

When he walked by the guest room, he noticed a dim light shining underneath the door, making him wonder if Annie was on her phone or had simply left on the closet light. Some people did that when in a strange place.

A groan sounded, followed by Annie's shrill voice. "No…"

He twisted the knob and burst through the door. Even without turning on the light, he could see her in the bed, her head shaking violently back and forth.

"Annie. Wake up. You're having a dream." He leaned over the bed and gently shook her shoulder.

Her eyes flew open and landed on him before blinking rapidly. Her arm shot out. "Get back."

He dodged the quick blow. "Annie, it's me. You had a dream. It's just a dream."

She glanced wildly around the room, and then her attention focused on him.

"Is everything all right?" Gabe stood in the open doorway in a T-shirt and a pair of pajama pants.

Riggs glanced back to Annie. "We're fine. I think she was just having a nightmare."

Selena peered around Gabe, then the two of them exchanged glances. His sister-in-law asked, "Can I do anything? Get you a warm glass of milk?"

Annie shoved her hair away from her face. "No, thanks. I'm fine. Sorry to wake you. Maybe I shouldn't have stayed here."

"We wouldn't have it any other way." Selena added, "Any friend of Riggs is a friend of ours."

After his brother and sister-in-law retreated to their room, Riggs waited until his brother's door closed before he sat on the edge of the bed. "Are you certain you're all right?"

She sat up in the bed and crossed her legs. She wore a pair of cotton shorts and T-shirt with his niece's baseball team logo that Selena must've loaned to her. Her flaming red hair was a mess. "Of course I'm fine. Just sorry I woke up the house."

"Do you do that often?"

"You mean have nightmares?" At his nod, she shook her head. "Not anymore. I used to, but I haven't in years."

His heart went out to her. "Care to share what this one was about?"

"Not really, but I will anyway." She sighed. "It's the children. Kay-Kay and Jonah. Well, part of it was them, but the rest was from a memory I recalled where two kids were being taken. My nightmare mixed Kay-Kay and Jonah up with the girls that got shoved into the van. Nice, huh?"

Riggs didn't respond to the rhetorical question but patted her hand instead. It seemed natural to want to hold her hand to comfort her, but she seemed agitated.

"Just like before, I started to do nothing to help, but then suddenly I knew something really terrible was going to happen. Even though the man scared me to death, I attempted to take them away from the abductor. The man tried to pull them from my grip. That's when you woke me up." She shivered.

"You know you saved Kay-Kay and Jonah, right? Without you, they'd still be in that house awaiting a terrible fate. Now they're safe with Josie."

She rubbed her forehead. "I know. I'll just feel better when they're back with their parents, and we find the house where they were being kept. I won't be able to sleep until the people behind the abductions are in prison."

He gave her a reassuring smile and patted her on the shoulder. "We'll find the holding house tomorrow."

"I'm sure you're right. The nightmare was probably brought on by me being preoccupied with the children."

"Are you going to be all right?" He hated to leave her alone. He'd like to stay with her, like sleep in the chair in the corner, but he doubted she'd appreciate the gesture. Besides, he didn't want Gabe and Selena to get the idea there was more to their relationship than there was.

"I'm fine. Go back to bed." She gave him a push. "I'm tougher than I look."

"I'll see you in the morning." He closed her door and headed back to his room. First thing tomorrow, he'd call the judge and get someone else in on this. Annie was right—they needed to find the other children, or they'd never have a moment's peace.

THIRTEEN

Embarrassment for having woken up the house consumed Annie. But more importantly, she couldn't erase the images of the nightmare from her mind. She knew there were more kids at that house. If her memory were correct, this would be the largest takedown she'd participated in.

Her biggest concern was this feeling of doom. Why did this case feel different? Was it just because she had amnesia and couldn't remember the details? Of course, she'd never suffered from a loss of memories before, so how would she know what was different and what was normal?

She stared at the ceiling for at least thirty minutes before finally deciding to get up.

Grabbing the iPad from the dresser that Selena had loaned her, she typed in the password and searched for the Bring the Children Home Project. With a click on the About tab, she read how the group worked in a coordinated effort with law enforcement agencies and other organizations. They were a group of highly trained volunteers who helped families bring missing children home or find the faith to cope with the loss. The page went on to give the background of their founder, Bliss Walker, and her credentials earned with the US Marshal Service.

The team members' page shared a photo and a limited description of each participant—title, job duties and qualifications. It was unnecessary to look up the information, for most of the details she recalled. The feeling of belonging warmed her, and she was glad she'd taken the time to look.

She closed out that tab and began to scan through articles on kidnappings. Some stories seemed vaguely familiar, but she couldn't recall details from any of the stories. That didn't mean she hadn't heard about the cases—in her profession, one heard about most incidents. After exploring the articles, she searched social media posts. Citizens were great about sharing information when a child went missing. Finally, after skimming about fifty posters of missing people ranging from newborn to the elderly, her eyes rested on Kay-Kay and Jonah's photos.

Seeing them on a missing-children poster made her heart ache. The post gave their ages and where they were last seen, as well as what they were wearing. Annie scrolled through the comments, many of which were praying, offering condolences or announcing that they'd shared the information. And then her eyes lit on a picture that someone by the name of Mike Romero had posted, saying police were interested in the silver sedan in the photo, as it was seen in the area shortly before the children went missing.

Annie stared at the car. It may've been the one at the farmhouse. The hubcaps were unique, in that the center had a red emblem that stood out against the silver.

Yes, she was positive that one was identical to the one parked outside in the drive.

The car was common and would be near impossible to locate. And this was near Fort Worth, a good five-hour drive from Palo Duro Canyon. No one would be looking for that vehicle around here. Maybe the police would have looked in the neighborhood surrounding the Ferrell house, or, if blessed, nearby cities and towns. But who was Annie fooling? Children were taken by relatives, or wandered off and got lost, or purposely ran away every day. Few were kidnapped by strangers. Except for those closest to the children, society became desensitized to the news.

Like sand sifting through an hourglass, more children went missing day after day. And with each passing day, she was drowning—sinking lower and lower and not able to find enough of these precious kids to make a difference. For the ones who ran away or were taken by relatives, she didn't know how to help except through more education or social programs.

But with child trafficking rings, you had to start at the top. Find the ones making the money. The sellers. The buyers. It was a horrible thing when children became a commodity. Only by stopping the ones at the top of the chain could a difference be made.

Annie laid the iPad beside her on the bed and bowed her head. "Please, Lord, help me do my part. Help me find the other kids. Not for my glory, but for Yours, and so these families can heal. Amen."

As soon as she was through with the prayer, the weight lifted slightly from her shoulders. She wasn't in this alone. God was on her side. So was Riggs. As was the Bring the Children Home Project. Even though

Annie felt alone at times, she knew it wasn't true. She just needed to do her part.

She'd start early in the morning, and hopefully Riggs would be with her. If not, she would go looking on her own. But she also knew how Bliss felt about the team. Her boss reminded them constantly to lean on the team and local law enforcement. "We need everyone home safely more than we need heroes and heroines."

It took Annie a while to understand the statement, but rescuing Kay-Kay and Jonah without her team had almost cost her, Riggs and the children their lives. As difficult as it was, Annie needed to listen and not go off on her own.

The next morning, Riggs called the judge.

"Hello?" The family friend's voice came out rough and groggy. "Who is this?"

"Judge, this is Riggs Brenner. I need to talk with you."

"Riggs?" His tone lightened. "What can I do for you? I assume it's important or you wouldn't be calling so early on a Saturday morning."

Riggs cringed. "I apologize for the hour, but it is important." He stood from the couch that he'd slept on, too wired to sit. "I've found myself in a bit of a situation and need advice."

"Are you in some kind of trouble?"

"Yes, but not trouble with the law. This is a little awkward, but I don't know how else to say it except be straight with you."

"I wouldn't have it any other way. Honesty is the best policy."

"Is Sheriff Rafe Ludlam trustworthy?"

"Ludlam? I believe so. He can be rough and has received some of the common complaints, like many others. Anyone in politics or law enforcement sets themselves up for people to be critical. You should know that."

"Yes, sir." There was no way to ask general questions without telling the judge what was going on. "A friend and I have been the targets of a couple of assailants, and we believe the attacks might be connected to a child kidnapping ring."

A heart-pounding second passed before the judge asked, "A kidnapping ring around here? Surely you jest. I would've heard about it."

"I'm afraid not." Maybe he'd made a mistake calling his friend. Of course, the judge may not have heard about it if no charges had been brought against anyone recently. He hated to tell his old friend the details because mentioning the word *amnesia* would bring them under scrutiny. "A couple of children were rescued close to my ranch, and it appears there are more children being kept at a holding house."

"What? I don't believe it."

The judge's tone turned defensive. Not that Riggs totally blamed him. Even though the crime was on the news every day, people didn't believe it happened in their own backyard. Without mentioning Annie by name or the amnesia, Riggs explained about finding her running from two armed men and them blowing up his house.

Silence greeted him, evidently Jacobs thinking it over. Finally, he asked, "What's the woman's name and why was she out there?"

He trusted the judge to keep her name protected, but

Riggs used Annie's undercover name. "Stormy Fowler. And she was trying to find the kids."

"Have you gone to the place she supposedly found them?"

Supposedly? "She can't remember the exact location. But we hope to search for the place soon."

"No, son, you're better off to let the authorities handle it, since you're no longer with the bureau. You said Ludlam knows. Have you told anyone else?"

Being reminded that he was no longer with the FBI hit Riggs in the gut. True, but it was a reminder of his failures. "I haven't. Not besides you."

"Okay. I'll make some calls to our local authorities. I'm sure hoping you're wrong about this, Brenner, but keep this under your hat."

"I'm not wrong, but I agree with the sentiment."

"Son, how well do you know this woman?"

He swallowed down annoyance. Why was the judge questioning him about her? "She's trustworthy."

"Okay. I hope you know what you're doing. You were always a smart one. That's why I wrote that recommendation letter when you wanted to join the FBI. I hope I eased your mind about Ludlam. Thanks for letting me know what's going on. You and your lady friend stay safe."

As Riggs disconnected the call, irritation crawled over him. He didn't appreciate being told to stay out of the way. And why bring up the recommendation letter? Almost like the judge was disappointed with the way Riggs turned out, or that he owed the judge? But what did Riggs expect? If he'd been in the judge's position, he might have had the same concerns.

After his conversation, he still hadn't learned more about the sheriff than before.

"Are you awake?" Annie's voice whispered from outside his door.

"I am. Come on in."

She stepped into the room dressed in denim shorts, a navy blue T-shirt and her hiking boots. Her flaming red hair stood out against the blue and was once again pulled back in a ponytail through the back of a white cap. Riggs couldn't help but notice how cute she looked. And he realized for the first time since talking with the judge how protective he'd become of Annie. Not only was she attractive, but smart and capable. She was trying to do good by rescuing kids. That was a mission he could get behind.

Before overhearing Josie tell her how impressed she'd been with Annie, Riggs had known she'd be good at her job. What he wouldn't do to have that desire to serve again. Even though she'd suffered with amnesia, she seemed to know what she wanted in life.

"I'm ready to go when you are," she said. "I'd like to see if I can remember the way to the holding house and to my Jeep."

Tension shot across his neck and shoulders. "I just talked with an old family friend who is a judge. He suggested we step back and let the local authorities do their job."

"No way." Her response was so sharp it startled him. "It *is* my job to find these children." Her face softened. "Our team works with the locals, but we don't just step out of the way. I'm trained. I know what I'm doing. I understand if you don't want to—"

Riggs held up his hand. "Wait."

She plowed right on like he hadn't spoken. "—help. I'll find the house while I wait for my team to arrive."

A smile came to his lips. "I get it. You're on a mission and can taste blood. Well, excuse that expression, but I understand. You feel you're close."

"I *am* close, and I'm familiar with the case. This is all our team does. We find children. I'm not criticizing local law enforcement, for they have a tough job, but they must be prepared for a wide range of crimes—from domestic abuse, theft, drugs and traffic crimes to murder. Not me. It's just about the kids. My boss constantly reiterates the importance of working with local law enforcement. But this judge, you say, wants us to stand back? The sheriff is the one to make that call. We can talk to him. Or better yet, my boss can contact him and get permission."

"I understand, Annie." He sighed. "You want to go to the ranch?"

"As in south of your ranch?"

"Yes, later. First, I need to check on my horses and cattle, and I'm supposed to meet investigators there to look at the scene and gather evidence. While there, I'll make certain those guys didn't cut my fence. I have a couple of cattle guards, but that doesn't mean the men used them."

Her eyes glistened. "Yes. I'd very much appreciate that."

When they walked out of the room, Selena was in the kitchen frying bacon and eggs, a funny expression on her face.

"Thanks for letting us stay." Riggs gave her a peck on the cheek. "Give Gabe my thanks."

His sister-in-law placed her hand on his bicep. "I'll

let him know." She whispered, "Please be careful, Riggs. Take care of your girl."

"She's not my girl."

Selena simply stared at him for several seconds. "I like her. But I worry about you."

"Don't. I know what I'm doing."

She nodded but didn't reply.

He gave her smile. "We're going."

"You're welcome back here tonight."

"Thanks. I'll let you know."

After he and Annie settled in his truck, his mind kept mulling over Selena's comments. Did it really appear like he was interested in Annie? Did Annie get that same impression?

He glanced at her as she stared out her window. What kind of fool was he making of himself? He didn't want anyone to think he was ready for a romantic relationship. There was simply no way he could allow Annie to search for those kids alone.

For all the danger and stress, though, he admitted this was the first time in years he'd felt alive.

FOURTEEN

The morning sun shined through the window of his rental truck. At this time of day, it was like all the danger had disappeared, but Riggs knew better. Annie, and maybe even him, would not be safe until these men were brought to justice.

He'd seen it in his days with the FBI. Criminals like this couldn't take chances of being caught. Witnesses or people who knew too much tended to die from unfortunate accidents, whether it be from a car crash or a house explosion. Or even a sudden heart attack. Unless an autopsy checked for certain drugs in the system, there were many ways to kill someone without being found out.

"That road right there." Annie pointed to a red dirt road that ran along the canyon.

Riggs slowed and turned. After learning who she was from Josie, Annie had seemed distant. He wanted to believe Annie, but his gut said she was holding back information. He didn't understand why. She couldn't have taken part in the crime, but he wondered what secrets she kept. It wouldn't be the first time he'd been surprised at people who had their hands dirty. He guessed that was one problem with being in law enforcement—you saw the bad in people. He'd like to wipe his memory clear and not see this side of humans. Maybe he should've been a rancher from the beginning. Live on a ranch and visit with family and neighbors occasionally.

But even that wouldn't have worked. Annie had brought trouble to his door, and he was glad he was trained.

"There. Turn by that tree."

He glanced her way. She'd been quiet on the trip from town. Her features were taut, her voice serious. A large mesquite tree stood to the right, and he pulled in beside it. "Does this look familiar?"

"I think so." She squinted as she looked out the passenger-side window. "All the roads look familiar, but it feels right."

"Good enough for me." Potholes littered the road, and he let off the accelerator, slowing to a safer speed. As he topped the rise, the path broke away. Yesterday's rain would make it easy to get stuck. He steered to the left. A huge mud hole appeared in the middle of the road, and he hit the gas. They smashed into the hole with a jolt. The truck slid sideways, but he kept the pedal down and soon they were on the other side.

A deep ditch stood on the right, and something reflected. He braked and came to a stop. A yellow Jeep Wrangler leaned to the side of the ditch.

"That's my Jeep." He'd no more stopped than she jumped out of his truck.

He got out and strode up beside her. Bullet holes riddled the side, and the back window was shot to pieces. Two tires were blown, causing it to lean.

"Ah. My Jeep. Look at it. I can't believe they shot it up." Her hand covered her mouth.

Riggs glanced at her.

"What?" She shrugged and then hurried down the ditch and opened the door.

"Doesn't look like the engine's been hit. If it weren't for the tires, you could drive it out."

She let out a sigh. "You're right. I'll still have to replace the windows. Do you know how long it took to save up for this vehicle? I had to drive a beater for two years just to come up with enough money to afford this."

"I do understand."

At his words, she looked up like realization dawned on her. "Oh, I'm sorry. I can't believe I just said that. You lost your home, and your truck is totaled. I shouldn't complain."

Riggs shook his head. "I know how it feels. My late wife, Claire, had wanted a classic Mustang, and I secretly saved forever to give her that car for her birthday the year our Macy Sue was born." He looked at into Annie's green eyes and saw a storm of emotion brewing. "I'm sorry for not telling you about them earlier. I figured you put it together after Gabe mentioned my wife and daughter."

"Yeah," she whispered.

"My wife loved that car, but the house explosion destroyed it. Because Claire and Macy Sue died, too, I barely acknowledged the loss of the car, except for wishing I had it because it'd been important to her." His throat grew tight, and he coughed to clear it. "I remember you mentioning how I hadn't said much about the loss of my cabin. When you lose the people closest to you, things don't matter as much."

"I'm so sorry, Riggs. I had no idea."

He took her hand in his. "I don't talk about them, mainly because their deaths were my fault."

"What do you mean?" Annie's brow wrinkled.

"It was our anniversary, and we had hired a sitter for Macy Sue so we could celebrate at a new Italian restaurant in town. But I was close to finishing a case, so I called Claire and canceled dinner, promising to make it up to her the next night. There was a gas leak we didn't know about, and the house exploded. No warning. No one should've been home."

"Oh, Riggs. Their deaths weren't your fault. Just a horrible accident."

He pulled her into his arms, clinging to her like his life depended on it. She wrapped her arms around his neck, and he laid his face on top of her head, feeling her warmth.

When she looked up at him, he didn't see any judgment there. He saw empathy and understanding, a tirade of emotions—none of them reproach.

He cupped her face and leaned in, pressing his lips against hers. He half expected her to pull away, but instead she kissed him back. Her touch sent sparks of electricity he hadn't felt in years. What was he doing? Annie would leave soon, and it wasn't fair to make false promises.

He leaned back and dropped his hands to his side. "Sorry."

She blinked, disappointment swirling in her gaze Her fingers went to her lips and stayed there before realization lit in her eyes. She looked away. "No need to apologize."

"Annie, I didn't mean it that way."

"Seriously. It's okay." She flushed. "We'll be going our separate ways soon. Now, let me see if there's anything in my Jeep that helps me." She dug through papers on the seats and some things on the floorboard.

He noticed she talked too fast, a clear sign she was upset.

She planted her hands on her hips. "Besides a few fast-food bags, there's nothing. I must've kept a cleaner vehicle than I expected. Wait." She leaned across the back seat and grabbed a folder from the passenger-side pocket.

He glanced over her shoulder as she flipped through a pile of handwritten papers.

"It's my notes on the Ferrell case." Her voice brimmed with what sounded like forced excitement. She continued to skim. "Yes. Just like Josie said, these are the addresses of the cars that had the first four letters of the license plate. Right here."

"Annie." He tried to take her hand in his, but she quickly pulled away.

Her eyebrows rose. "I said I'm fine."

Riggs let out a deep sigh. He hadn't meant to anger her. Anything but that. He hated the thought of hurting her. His feelings were in a tangled mess.

His gaze landed on a name and address scribbled down, and his chest tightened. He knew that property.

"I must've planned to call the team if it checked out. You can see where I marked the other three addresses from my list. The kids have got to be there. Fifty-six ten Bois D'arc County Road. How close is that?" She glanced up, a clip to her voice. "What's wrong?"

"I know this place. Mostly used as a deer lease or a retreat for businessmen."

She straightened. "Do you know the owner?" When he hesitated, she scrolled down her notes. "A Henrietta Jacobs? That's the name on the property taxes record."

"I know of her."

"Looks like she's ninety-two. I'd hope a lady of that age was not behind the kidnapping and the attacks." Annie continued her chatter, and her earlier bite softened. "Probably the ringleader is a relative or even someone who leased the land for hunting, but the owner doesn't realize what's taking place on her own property."

Henrietta was Judge Chadwick Jacobs's mother. Riggs didn't want to jump to conclusions, but this didn't look good. And Annie could be right. Hopefully, the land had been leased to someone else as a ruse for hunting, and the owners didn't know what was taking place.

"Let's go check it out."

Riggs glanced at his cell phone. "We need to meet investigators at the ranch. Then we'll drive to the address."

"Can't you tell the sheriff's department you're running late?"

"No. And besides, that'll give your team time enough to get here." He looked at her. "How far away are they?"

"I'd say four to five hours, besides Josie. Most live in the Dallas Metroplex."

"Good. Let's go to the ranch."

Her shoulders dropped, and her lips tightened. "Fine. I know you're right. I'm just ready to save those kids."

"I know you are."

Annie's hand gripped the grab handle above her head as Riggs drove over the rough canyon roads.

The truck bounced with each dip. "Hang on. The rain washed part of the road away."

She wasn't worried about the road. Her mind bounced between the children and Riggs's kiss. His confession of guilt for the deaths of his wife and daughter had astounded her. She had sensed there was a reason he lived in seclusion, and for his unrelenting determination to protect Kay-Kay and Jonah. It all made sense now.

But he still didn't know about her family—her secret. Was there a reason to tell him about her father? She'd soon be back in Liberty, engrossed in her work, and wouldn't see him again. No good would come from telling Riggs now. They'd find the children, hopefully today, and then she'd be gone.

If they were to find the children, she needed to concentrate her efforts on them. Her anxiety rose at each passing second the children were in the hands of criminals. The investigation could wait. Actually, a report needed to be made and all the data collected before evidence disappeared. Even the storm had probably washed some of it away.

She'd called Bliss at Bring the Children Home Project to give her an update after finding the Jeep and asked for backup. It seemed to take forever to arrive at the ranch. Annie had thought it quicker to enter the back side and drive across his ranch, but Riggs had claimed there were some areas that were impassable, and even though taking the main road was longer, it was quicker.

Honey and Jack munched grass near their pen, their heads coming up as they approached the barn. "The horses are back."

Riggs nodded. "Most times they'll run for home, so no surprise. And there are my cattle." He pointed at a herd of black animals on a hill in the distance and glanced at the clock on the dash. "The investigators aren't due for another twenty minutes. Let's check on the cows after I unsaddle the horses."

Annie remained quiet as he got out to pen the horses. Grabbing their reins, he led both animals into their wooden enclosure, and she watched with fascination as he stripped them of their saddles and gear. Even now, Honey held still for Riggs, while Jack stamped his foot and tossed his head. She smiled at the difference in the horses' demeanors.

After he made two trips into the barn carrying the gear, Riggs strode to the truck and climbed in. "Okay. Ready."

Normally she would've enjoyed looking at the herd, for she'd always wanted to be raised around animals, but not today. The longer she was away from the holding house, the more her stomach churned. "What if because I rescued Kay-Kay and Jonah, the criminals sent the other children away to cover their tracks? What if the kids are gone by the time we get there?"

He looked over at her before turning his attention back to the path. For a moment, he remained silent as he drew near a herd of about a hundred cows. Finally, he said, "I understand your concern. We have a few minutes. I'll keep my conversation with the investigators short—five, ten minutes, tops. Then we'll drive to the place and wait for backup so that we can keep an eye on them. Will that work?"

She wanted to go now, but she nodded.

He counted the animals aloud as he eased around the herd. After making several rounds, he finally asked, "Where's her calf?"

Suddenly alert, Annie noted several calves in the group. As they drove around, the cattle bunched in a circle and drew close to the truck. "Why are they doing that?"

He smiled. "I feed hay and range cubes in the wintertime. They think I'm going to feed them."

"Aw. That's sad."

He shook his head. "Nah. They have plenty of grass and water right now with all the rain. Some years we don't get much rain at all."

"That can't be good."

"Can be stressful. My first year ranching was particularly dry, and I had to haul hay in from Kansas."

"Isn't that expensive?"

"Yep."

Two ears twitched from among the short prairie grass. "There." She pointed. "Is that it?"

As the truck neared, the black calf jumped to its feet, darted toward the herd and found what Annie assumed was his mama.

"They're all here." He turned the truck around and headed for the barn.

They stopped in the drive, and her gaze landed on the ruins of his house. For the first time, she noticed a whiskey barrel full of flowers, apparently untouched by the flames and a freestanding cedar porch swing under a juniper tree. Rugged but beautiful. The image of Riggs caring for Kay-Kay and Jonah played through her mind. "You have a beautiful place. What a great place to raise a family." The words were out before she could stop them.

His head jerked, and the color drained from his face.

"I'm sorry." She couldn't believe she'd just said that. "I wasn't thinking."

Riggs nodded but didn't respond.

Awkwardness settled in the quiet of the cab and her heart squeezed, hating that she was the reminder of his pain. The man beside her had lost so much. Maybe that's why she could relate to him in her own way. What she wouldn't have done to have a father who cared for her like Riggs had for Kay-Kay and Jonah, who weren't even his own children. That's what she was going to miss about him most. The feeling he'd understood her.

Or would he? He still didn't know her identity. Would he feel the same if he knew she was Nelson Craddick's offspring?

He pulled around the back side of the barn and parked in front of the horse pens, she supposed so he wouldn't destroy evidence—he must not want to mark up the area with more tire tracks. He glanced at the clock on the dashboard. "The investigators should be here soon. I hope they don't have trouble getting through the canyon."

"Do you think they will?"

"As long as they stay on the main drive, they won't. But it doesn't take much to get a vehicle stuck. It's happened to me several times. That was one reason I built where I did. Concrete mixers or big vehicles can't make the climb and sharp turns to other parts of canyon."

"Is there no other way?"

"Unless you want to helicopter supplies in or spend an obscene amount of money to build improved roads, no."

"I've never thought of that. I assumed if you had a 4x4 truck, all was good."

"I wish." He looked at the clock again.

She grabbed the door handle. "Can I pet your horses while we wait?"

"Sure." He opened his door, too.

They both got out and headed toward the pen. Anything was better than sitting in the truck, which made her more antsy. Annie rested her foot on the bottom rung, and Honey trotted to her. She rubbed a hand down her neck, the soft hair tickling her fingers. The mare neighed in response. Jack moved closer but stayed out of reach. "Oh, come on. I won't hurt you."

She plucked a handful of grass and held it out. Honey immediately took it from her and munched. No matter how many times she held it out to Jack, he refused to take it. He trotted back and forth across the pen. Annie wished she could release some of her energy that way.

Riggs checked his watch again. "I hope they don't have trouble getting around in the canyon."

"Surely they have four-wheel-drive vehicles."

He nodded. "The sheriff's department does. I don't know about the investigators." After a second, he said, "I'm going to check up by the rockslide. The sheriff told me they would meet me at the house, but I wonder if they stopped at my truck and decided to take pictures there first."

She sighed. "I hope not. I don't want to wait any longer. I should've rented a vehicle, and then I could go find the house while you wait."

His cheek twitched. "Seriously? You can wait for me. I'm just as eager to get out of here as you. You want to ride with me?"

"Nah. You go ahead. I'll stay here in case investigators show up here. Hey, can you call them? Do you have reception?"

"Nope. I've already checked."

"That's annoying." Her lip twisted. "I don't see how you stand it."

"I normally have the booster, remember? But it must be plugged in."

"Okay. Get going." She playfully shoved his shoulder.

He nodded and said, "I'll be right back."

As Annie watched him, she realized how blessed she was to have him in her life right now. He'd literally been a lifesaver. His black truck climbed up the hill and disappeared over the rise.

An eerie loneliness rained down on her.

Maybe she should've gone with him. But that was silly. Riggs wasn't leaving, and she still had her weapons on her.

The horses went back to eating grass, and a breeze blew across the canyon floor, kicking up dust.

The place really was beautiful. She'd meant what she said to Riggs earlier, that this would be a great place to raise a family. Peaceful and rugged. She could imagine watching the sunset from a porch. Well, at least once he rebuilt his house.

A rumble sounded in the distance. Good grief. What were the investigators driving?

But as the noise grew, she realized it wasn't a vehicle. No, it was something much bigger. And it was coming from the direction Riggs had gone.

FIFTEEN

Riggs watched Annie in his rearview mirror as he topped the hill. He couldn't help but notice she stared after him. A slight smile crossed his lips as she disappeared from his sight. He couldn't help but think of the kiss.

The fact she had kissed him back surprised him. Was there a chance for a relationship in his life? Was he ready?

Not just any relationship, but with Annie. Since the night he found her running from gunmen in the canyon, he hadn't been able to think of anything else. They made an excellent team. But would she want to live in the middle of nowhere? Or would she expect him to move to Liberty, north of Dallas? He didn't want to make a move in her direction if he wasn't certain.

Right now, he just didn't know.

Like her, he was ready to get to the farmhouse. The Bring the Children Home Project members would be here in a few hours, hopefully along with the Sanderson County Sheriff's Department.

He traveled the winding road, keeping an eye out for the investigators. They should be here by now. A funny feeling settled in his stomach. Surely nothing was wrong. There'd be no reason for concern. Judge Chadwick had thought there was nothing alarming about Sheriff Ludlam.

Doubt plagued Riggs. Even though he hadn't seen the house or the children, after working with the FBI, he knew kidnapping rings like this could have deep criminal roots. Money lured even the most prestigious of men. He'd learned not to be surprised at who might get caught up in a crime, and many times, the people at the top never got caught or supplied enough evidence to be brought down.

As he approached the pile of rocks, his stomach knotted. The landslide had demolished the vehicle, but at least he had full coverage. Hopefully, insurance companies didn't list rockslides as an exclusion. He climbed to the ledge above the slide so he could get a good look. The investigators were not in sight. Again, that funny feeling that something was wrong. Careful not to track up the ground, he took as few steps as possible and surveyed the area. The rain must've washed away the footprints or tire tracks.

There was no other obvious evidence, like a large rock bar that would pry up a huge rock to cause the slide. Not that he expected something so obvious.

A rumble sounded. What was that? He looked up and shielded his eyes from the sun's rays with his hand.

A helicopter flying much too low. His heart thumped in his chest. Please tell him this wasn't the gunmen. But as the copter approached, an assault rifle pushed through the opening of the cockpit.

Who were these people?

At a full-out run, he went down the canyon wall,

sliding and falling. Small trees and brush bit into him and beat his body.

Bullets peppered the ground all around him. Hunkering behind a slab of rock, he fired shots at the cockpit. Doubtful he could hit anyone at this distance, but maybe it'd make them leery.

To his surprise, the machine didn't make another sweep, but continued west—toward the barn and Annie.

Oh no. He raced to his truck. He never should've left her. Please, God, help him get there in time!

Annie paced back and forth between the barn and the remains of the house. Twice, she even trekked up the hill for a better look, trying to see if she could spot the investigators coming this way. Besides the cattle grazing, there was nothing moving.

She hadn't heard the rumble of an engine again.

Restless with energy, she couldn't stand the waiting. Why did they have to wait for investigators? Surely Riggs could explain the locations without having to point them out. If they had questions, they could call him later. Right?

But even as the thoughts raced through her mind, she knew she was being impatient—something she'd always struggled with. They couldn't go in until her team was there, anyway.

Suddenly, a strange noise arose again on the horizon. What was that?

Jack raised his head and trotted across his pen.

Almost sounded like a vehicle, but too loud. Was it Waylon and Sonny?

A dark shadow flashed across the land. She automatically ducked as a black helicopter whizzed low in the canyon.

Bullets sprayed the ground, sending Annie seeking cover back in the barn.

She was well hidden, but the shock that the criminals would attack with a *helicopter* was unbelievable. She must've made someone extremely angry by taking the kids and finding their hiding place.

Someone with a lot of power and money.

Had they spotted Riggs? Had they been shooting at him?

Concern swirled through her. He had to be okay.

Careful to stay in the shadows, she took another glimpse outside. The helicopter was out of sight, but she heard the rotating blades, telling her it must be overhead and turning around. The whirling grew louder and echoed through the canyon.

The copter hovered before landing on the canyon floor, only fifty yards away. Two men jumped out with rifles.

Her heart raced. She had two guns on her person, but that didn't equip her to handle this assault. She would be a sitting duck if they found her in the barn. But there was no other hiding place, and they were bound to check inside the building. If she positioned herself in the loft, maybe she could defend herself.

The area outside provided little cover, making her think twice about running for it. Part of her wanted to make a mad dash, hoping to lead the men away from the area in case Riggs returned, but their guns would shoot too far.

Instead of turning toward the barn, one man, bald with an athletic build, jogged east, toward where Riggs had gone. They must've seen him. The other man was wearing a black cap and shirt and was lean and quick. He sprinted toward her, carrying a rifle. Neither man was Waylon or Sonny. How many people were after them? Her heart constricted. Backing to the other side of the opening to gain a better view, her gaze followed the road, searching for Riggs's truck. Surely he'd heard the helicopter's whirling blades.

The man sprinted up the first hill that Riggs had gone up.

Riggs was a capable fighter, and she had to trust he could handle his man. Her attention turned to the gangly man zigzagging her way. At this distance, she couldn't tell what kind of rifle he carried, but no doubt, the weapon was more powerful than either of her guns.

Not wanting to get in a fight carrying the smaller weapon, she decided to take him out before he found her. Moving behind a massive wooden beam for protection, she eased the barn door open just enough to give her an obstructed view. She took aim.

The man's wild movement across the rough terrain made him a challenging target.

Wait. Let him get closer.

If she missed, he'd realize her location and pummel the barn with bullets. It'd be next to impossible to compete with his firepower. Letting out a breath, she aimed and squeezed the trigger.

Boom.

The skinny man jerked but didn't fall. He darted for a nearby tree and then opened fire. Bullets sprayed the barn, one hitting the post she hid behind, and beams of sunlight shone through the holes in the wall. Wood splinters stabbed her. She dropped to her haunches and crouched behind the post, making herself as small as possible. The barn door blew inward from the force of blows.

She peeked around the corner and saw him hurrying her way. He let off another round as he ran, but his aim was high. He had an obvious limp now.

Staying down, she discharged more fire.

Suddenly, he jerked and fell to the ground. He scrambled back to his feet long enough to dive into the brush.

She stood still and watched. The man could hope to shoot her if she came into the open. After a moment, she detected a patch of black in motion. Finally, he crawled back up the hill in the opposite direction of the helicopter.

Was there a man with the machine, or had one of the gunmen been the pilot? A lot of personal helicopters were only two-seaters, but this one had appeared larger. Seriously, what did she know about personal aircraft, anyway? She didn't see movement through the tinted windows.

One last glance at the empty horizon and her concern for Riggs grew. She would check out the helicopter, and once it was clear, she'd go looking for him.

Please, Lord, help me.

Securing Waylon's pistol in her pocket and her own Sig Sauer in her hand, she dashed out of the barn. She stumbled over a chunk of wood debris from the earlier house explosion as she sprinted across the flat ground and dropped to her knee. Quickly, she scrambled back up and hit the ground running. The lanky gunman who had disappeared in the brush hadn't shot again. She weaved in and out of the brush for cover, hoping she wouldn't get caught in the open. Heaving deep breaths, she ran with all her might across the canyon floor. A cramp stabbed at her side, but she kept moving. Keeping her eyes trained on the window as she neared the helicopter, she searched for movement inside but saw none.

Only ten yards away.

She drew a deep breath and stopped. The consistent boisterous swirling from the revolving blades pulsated in her ears, and the wind was like a humongous fan blowing toward the ground, kicking up dirt. As she reached for the door handle, something moved from inside.

Annie's heart exploded as she yanked open the door. The pilot's eyes grew enormous, showing she had surprised him as much as he had her. Using the moment to her advantage, she grabbed the man's arm and yanked him out as he reached for what she assumed was a gun.

The man tried to keep his balance but only managed to slow his fall. He landed on her, knocking her to the ground. She kept her grip on her gun, but he had a hold of it, too. In one swift move, he pulled the trigger.

Fire burned along the bicep of her good arm. She returned shots, hitting him in his side.

Pain lit up his face as his hands clutched the wound.

A glance up the hill showed the bald gunman running her way. Shoving the throbbing of her arm to the back of her mind, pure willpower allowed her to climb into the helicopter. It would be so much easier if the thing simply had a key in the ignition she could turn off. It'd been years since Annie had been in a helicopter, but her dad had taken her on a ride one time. He'd been in the air force before receiving a dishonorable discharge.

The bald man was closing in. She had to hurry.

Not being able to recall anything about the instrument panel and how things worked, she did the only thing she could think of—she stepped out of the door onto the landing skid and took aim at the control panel. Her first shot was at the throttle. The recoil caused an explosion of pain, and the pistol slipped from her hands and tumbled to the ground. The man grew closer in her peripheral vision.

She tried not to panic as she scrambled for the weapon and fired. The dash exploded, but the machine continued to run. Stepping back so she wouldn't get hit by a ricocheting bullet, she riddled the dash with her Sig. Twelve rounds and finally, the engine stopped. The blades slowed, and the sounds grew quieter.

She aimed her empty Sig at the man. "Stop."

He stutter-stepped, and his gaze went to the pilot on the ground.

Her other gun was still in her pocket, but there was no time to retrieve it.

The bald man smiled as his gun came up. "Got yourself into a pickle, didn't you, missy?"

Oh, this was not good. Where was Riggs? Her eyes scanned the horizon but didn't see him anywhere.

The guy had stopped ten yards away, too far for her to disarm him. Evidently feeling safe that backup had arrived, the pilot attempted to get to his feet.

Two to one was not good odds.

Riggs had avoided being shot by the gunman, but he might not be so blessed next time. He'd seen the man disappear over the top of the hill a few minutes ago. Suddenly, the sound of the chopper quieted before all went silent. His heart pumped with adrenaline.

He got in his truck and tore across the land toward

Annie. As he barreled through the brush, he caught sight of the helicopter. Then his gaze landed on Annie. A man had his weapon aimed at her, and another struggled to get to his feet. Riggs sucked in a breath. There was no way she could take them both on. He stopped his truck in the brush, stepped out and dropped to a knee. It was important for the men to know that she wasn't alone.

Purposefully, he aimed to the left of the tall man and fired. The shot echoed through the canyon, and both men turned back to get his location.

Riggs remained stock-still behind the juniper, hoping they wouldn't spot him.

One man shouted, "Get him."

Annie took advantage of the distraction by dropping and rolling under the chopper. She grabbed the gun from her pocket, took aim and fired.

The man in the black shirt fell to the ground, holding his knee.

The other man disappeared behind a slab of rock. The area was littered with brush and cedar trees, making for sufficient cover. Riggs got back in his truck and charged toward the copter with his eyes on full alert.

Annie crawled out on the other side of the helicopter.

As he neared the place where the man had disappeared, Riggs slowed. With his gun ready, he got out, then peered around. The man was gone. Careful and watching to make certain the guy wasn't lying in wait, Riggs finished making his way to Annie and the helicopter on foot.

She held up her hands. "Where did that guy go? I shot him in the leg. Look, there's blood." She pointed to a small rock.

"Both guys got away. Without the chopper, they'll be looking for a way out to recuperate." He glanced at the man on the ground. "The pilot?"

She nodded. "He's alive but not doing so well."

Riggs walked over to him. "What's your name?"

The man's eyes fluttered open, and his jaw was tight. "Doesn't matter. But I have nothing to do with what's going on. I'm just a pilot."

"If you're being paid by a bunch of criminals, then you're guilty. We'll get you help soon."

The man paled, and his breathing slowed. He was slipping away.

"If you're not involved, then help us. Who's behind all this? Who are these guys?"

The pilot shook his head. "The top. High places. Can't be touched."

Riggs didn't believe that. Authorities could bring down anyone with the right evidence, but he'd seen it happen when someone with money could pay off enough people. "Mister, I think you're right. You were just the pilot. Help us. Tell me who's behind this or why?"

"Big ring. But the person…"

Bam.

A shot rang out and hit the pilot in the side of his chest. Both Riggs and Annie hit the dirt, taking cover.

Riggs rolled and fired several rounds in succession toward the area he thought the shot had come from.

When Riggs looked up, the pilot was dead.

What had they gotten themselves into when it was more important to stop the pilot from talking than to shoot either of them?

* * *

Even though she knew it was useless, Annie checked the pilot's wrist for a pulse. There wasn't one. She glanced up as Riggs approached her. "He's dead."

Riggs looked at the destroyed instrument panel of the helicopter. "Looks like you disabled it?"

"I would guess so."

He sighed and looked back in the direction the men had disappeared. "We need to keep an eye out for the two gunmen. If they don't have transportation, they could circle back and try to take us out. And if they connect with their leader, backup could be here shortly. I'm hoping they don't have any better connection than we do."

"That thought crossed my mind, too."

"Doesn't look like the sheriff's deputy or investigators are going to show up." Riggs glanced at his watch. "They'd should've already been here."

She released a big pent-up breath. "I was thinking the same thing. Like this was a setup."

He frowned and rubbed the back of his neck. "I don't want to believe that, but it's looking like someone in law enforcement is involved."

"If the sheriff is involved, then who can we trust? You're not going to call them to report this, are you?"

"I probably should, but I think I'll hold off. Just in case…"

Even as she noted the unease in Riggs's expression, she continued. "The only ones I know aren't involved are members of my team."

The men had gone in the opposite direction toward the mouth of the canyon, but she didn't want to take chances in case one or both circled back.

Riggs said, "I'm going to check out the chopper."

"Thanks." She made certain both of her weapons were loaded and continued to watch for the men to return. She thought they were safe for now, but she always needed to be prepared. Her head throbbed, and her injured arm ached.

Riggs stepped out and let the door close.

"Did you find anything useful?"

"Not really. There's a map of the area, but no locations noted. I found paperwork that indicated our pilot was thirty-eight-year-old David Augustus. Does the name ring a bell?"

"No." She shook her head. "Anything else?"

"I didn't go through all the paperwork, but I found a box of clothes and children's supplies in the back." He frowned. "Appears like they planned for child passengers. I don't like the way this looks."

Her body ached from running for their lives, and the graze of the bullet on her bicep didn't help. At least the bandage covering her stitches was still secure. She sagged against the helicopter. She'd sleep for a year if she ever lay down to rest. But even as she dreamed, she knew it couldn't be. Not until the kids were safe in their parents' care and they found the other children—if they hadn't been moved.

Annie rested her hands on her hips. "I'm ready to go. I don't want to give the sheriff or anyone else time to make another hit."

"I agree. Let's get out of here."

"Riggs…"

His eyes connected with hers, and he waited for her to continue.

"I don't know what triggered my memory loss or

how I got Kay-Kay and Jonah from their abductors, but whatever we find, know that I appreciate everything you've done to help. I couldn't have survived without you."

A small smile creased the side of his mouth. "I don't mind. Remember, I used to do this for a living. But Annie…" He looked like he was trying to figure out the next words, for the pause was too long. "We need to be going."

Disappointment hit her. She had the feeling that was not what he'd planned to say. As they walked back to his truck, she watched him. He'd been hurt by the loss of his wife and daughter. Annie wished there was a way she could help him heal. But what did she know about assisting a person with their past?

She couldn't even handle her own family's failures.

SIXTEEN

The red farmhouse gleamed in the afternoon sun, causing Annie to shield her eyes with her hand. "That's it. That's the house."

Riggs sighed. "Are you certain?"

"Yes." Her heart constricted at the sight. If they did the job right, by this time tomorrow the children would be safe in the custody of the authorities and ready to reunite with their families. "I'll call the team to let them know we're here."

Three bars. Yes! She would never take good connection for granted again.

"Bliss Walker."

She put the phone on speaker. "This is Annie. We're positioned outside the house on Bois D'arc Road. I'll send you the address."

"Annie, I know you're anxious to rescue these children, but I don't need to remind you to wait for your team members and the sheriff's department. Two members are headed your direction, less than an hour from you. I've called the Sanderson County Sheriff's Department."

She glanced at Riggs and drew a deep breath. One

time Annie had gone in five minutes early to rescue a child, and even though everything turned out all right, her boss had been livid. "Yes, ma'am. Stick to the rules."

"That's right. The rules are there to keep everyone safe."

"Yes." Annie hated that Riggs could hear the reprimand. And she knew her boss would want to know why she'd saved the kids without backup, but she simply didn't remember. What if she never recalled? She didn't want to mention this morning's attack for fear Bliss would have them stand back, but she respected her boss too much to hold back. "We endured another assault this morning."

Silence. Then Bliss asked, "Were you or your partner hurt?"

Partner? As in Riggs? That had a nice ring to it. "No injuries. Just a graze from a bullet that didn't break the skin."

"I'll expect a full report later."

"Yes, ma'am."

"Keep in touch." Her boss paused. "And Annie. I'm glad you're better. You're doing a good job."

A smile crossed her lips. "Thank you." After she clicked off, she noticed Riggs staring at her.

"I like her. I like the whole Bring the Children Home concept. If you're ever in the area, you can always count on me to search for missing children."

"I figured that." And she knew it was true. He was the type of man you could depend on.

"I almost wished Bliss hadn't called the sheriff's department, though," he said. "I don't trust Sheriff Rafe Ludlam now."

"Yeah. Me neither. But without proof, I'm certain my boss would've called them anyhow."

Riggs pulled farther into the field, to the north side of the place. She noticed he kept his speed down, probably so his tires wouldn't kick up dust. He stopped in a low-lying area that was surrounded by short, scraggly mesquite trees. He rolled down the windows and killed the engine. "We should be well hidden."

Even though there was a slight breeze, the temperature was a dry one hundred degrees. Sweat beaded across her lip, and she was glad for the shade.

"Are you okay?" he asked.

She looked at him. "Yeah. Just need to slow the adrenaline when I know the kids are so close. I can't stand them being in hands of vile people another second. Patience is something I've always struggled with."

"I know what you mean, but restraint will save your life and theirs. How's your arm?"

"You mean the stitches or where the bullet grazed me?" At his scowl, she smiled. "Both are fine. The bullet burned more than it damaged me. Never even bled."

"Good."

She could only see the front of the house from her position. Anyone could come and go from the back, and they'd totally miss it. "Can you see the backyard?"

"Not really."

"Come on. Let's move closer."

"I don't want them to see the reflection of my truck. We're better off to move on foot. Put your cell phone on silent."

Annie did as he suggested and climbed out of the vehicle. "I'll stay hidden, but I want to see what's going on. I'd like to know that the children are still there."

"Fine. But stay under the cover of the trees. We don't want to blow this."

"Agreed." She stayed low and trekked across the rough terrain, keeping close to the mesquite. She couldn't remember how good the security system had been, but they'd be safer assuming it was decent. Did they always keep someone stationed outside?

A child's voice rose above the wind.

Annie's head fell forward to her chest with relief. A woman's voice carried their way before it drifted to silence. A new barbwire fence stretched out in front of them, and Riggs knelt on his haunches beside her.

She looked around. "I think this is where I observed the home before. There's still a few prints."

"I noticed that."

"It's the perfect hiding place with the line of trees blocking us. We can stay here unobserved." What had happened that caused her to go in early for Kay-Kay and Jonah without backup? Even if she saw a good opportunity, she knew better.

Riggs's gaze went over her shoulder. "Don't look now, but we have company."

Annie looked behind them. A red cloud grew from the road they'd just traveled. As it neared, a van emerged and swung into the entrance. "This is not good."

The van had tinted windows and tore down the drive, stopping on the side of the house. Two men got out, and a man who looked about forty years old came out from inside the home and met them.

She whispered, "Can you hear them?"

"No." Riggs touched her shoulder, as if reminding her to stay still.

Her dad had used a van. He could transport several

kids at once, and the dark windows made it easy to conceal his activities. The thought made her sick. After becoming a part of the Bring the Children Home team, she'd learned the children were moved mostly at night. So that was good. Maybe if these guys had any intentions of transporting the kids, it would be later. And by then it would be too late.

Her team would help secure the children before transferring them.

"Are you ready?" someone from the house yelled.

Annie couldn't see whoever called, for they were under the cover of the porch. Was Waylon or Sonny here? Or either of the men from the helicopter? She didn't know how severe their injuries were.

"Yes. We're ready anytime you are," the man in the van answered.

She looked at Riggs. "Are they planning to take the kids now?"

"I don't know," he whispered. "Patience."

Her heart picked up pace. "We can't let them take the kids anywhere. We'll lose them forever."

"Calm down. We won't let them out of our sight."

She grabbed his arm. "I'm moving closer so we can hear what they're saying. If they plan on leaving with the children, I need to let my team know. That would change everything."

Crouching down, Annie stayed low as she wound her way through the brush and closer to the barbwire fence. Riggs was right behind her. When they came to the fence, she stopped.

Another man came out of the house and visited with the first man, both strangers. They appeared to be whispering to each other.

Riggs touched her shoulder. "Don't move. They're on alert."

Annie realized this but refrained from saying anything more. She rested on her knee so she wouldn't lose her balance and draw attention to the movement. For a couple of minutes, people came and went from the house, and their voices no longer carried to them. Annie wondered if the men had purposely lowered their voices or if the wind had slightly changed directions.

Finally, all the men went inside the home. She double-checked to make sure no one hung around the outbuildings, but she didn't see anyone. Not unless one or more men hid inside the structures.

She said, "What do you think is going on?"

"I don't know, but I don't like it." He pulled his gun from its holster and checked it before returning. Annie did the same with hers.

Quietly, she checked her cell phone for any messages from her team. There were none.

The children's voices from earlier could no longer be heard. It was close to the lunch hour, so it was possible they were eating their noon meal or were being put down for a nap. The noonday heat sent sweat trickling down her back. She refrained from wiping her brow so as not to catch the attention of the guards.

Seven or eight more minutes slowly ticked by with no sounds or movement. "You want to move closer?"

Riggs shook his head. "Let's wait for backup. No need to pull the trigger early."

"I wouldn't say that." The strange male voice coming from behind them had them jumping to their feet.

Two men Annie had never seen before pointed assault rifles at them. Her chest squeezed, and her blood pumped through her ears. The bigger of the two smiled, his yellow teeth staring back at her. "Toss your weapons away."

Riggs and she exchanged glances before they both dropped their guns in the dirt.

"The boss wants to see you two. Don't try anything, and I might let you make it to the house without getting shot. This way." The big man nodded.

An open gate that Annie hadn't seen stood a few yards on the other side of the trees. All four of them filed through, the smaller man leading the way. Annie was careful to keep her hands where they could see them. She'd dealt with criminals like this before, and this wasn't the time to make a move. But she kept a close distance in case an opportunity arose to where she could disarm one of them.

The men were careful and alert, keeping out of reach. Almost like they could read their intentions. Her muscles tightened as she moved up the wooden porch, realizing the window to act was vanishing with each step. She glanced to the right, searching for a way to escape.

The big guy shoved her in the back, causing her to trip. She regained her balance before her face slammed into the door frame. "Don't try anything, missy."

The old home had probably been built in the 1950s—it had the large kitchen that was common during the period. Voices emerged from a back room. Annie wanted to turn around to see if Riggs was trying to tell her anything, but there simply no time. The men kept propelling them through the kitchen and down the hallway.

A woman dressed in shabby jeans and a faded T-shirt suddenly exited a side room, and her gaze connected with Annie's. A mole marked her cheek, and she had dark blond hair and wide eyes. Annie had seen that lady before, but she didn't know from where. Before Annie could get a second look, the woman scurried away.

Maybe she had seen her when she rescued Kay-Kay and Jonah. But that didn't feel right.

An empty living room, sparsely furnished with leather furniture, appeared on the right. The door to the left was open, and the man stopped in the hallway, blocking her path. "In there."

Before she had time to react, he shoved her into the room. She'd learned a long time ago not to give bad guys the satisfaction of acting weak or begging, but also not to present herself with a challenge. Just appearing calm and obedient was the best policy. At least it had been so far.

The lights were off, and the curtains drawn. A large desk dominated the middle of the room. The older man behind the oak piece of furniture looked up.

Annie's lungs froze, barely able to keep a gasp from escaping.

Her father stared back at her with dark, dangerous eyes.

Memories flooded her. Not only from her childhood, but the events that took place when she rescued the kids two nights ago. After searching the property to see if the car from the camera footage was there, Annie had located the car. On her way to her Jeep to call her team, she had heard a child quietly sobbing. Seeing no one else outside, she drew near the house and heard a man yell from inside for someone to find the girl. He threatened he'd beat the child along with her caregiver since this was the third time the girl had run away.

Annie found Kay-Kay holding Jonah behind the

bushes in the front of the house. She told Kay-Kay she was there to take her home, and the girl agreed to go with her. As they were sliding along the side of the house, Annie got a glimpse at the back of a man in a window who was throwing his hands into the air, complaining to someone on a video call. She recognized the man on the screen as Judge Chadwick Jacobs.

She had realized this kidnapping ring reached higher levels than believed. The man seated at the desk turned around. *Nelson Craddick. Her father.*

Grabbing Kay-Kay's hand and clinging to Jonah, she had run to her Jeep.

Currently, she stared at him. The man had aged. Wrinkles lined his face, and his rough complexion showed alcohol or drug use. Even though his shoulders hunched, his eyes were bright and alert. He'd not be easy to take down. He hadn't survived this long by being careless, and she needed to buy time until backup arrived.

Annie had prepared for this moment since the day she witnessed her father kidnap two girls. Her blood chilled. She'd waited for this day for most of her life.

Riggs stared at the older man behind the desk. Nelson Craddick. He been on the FBI's Most Wanted list for several years and Riggs's partner, Clayton McCarthy, had actively worked the case for many months. Craddick was extremely dangerous and well connected.

This was not good. Backup needed to show up soon. Craddick had remained hidden too long to be taken unaware. He wouldn't waste time keeping them as prisoners.

Did Annie sense the danger they were in?

Her face had turned white as a sheet, her body stiff and straight, making the pressure of saving her even heavier. Emotions danced in her eyes as her gaze bored into the man at the desk, a strange look on her face—more than just fear.

Riggs calculated the time in his head. The Bring the Children Home members and the sheriff's department should be here within the next thirty minutes. But could he hold off the bad guys that long? And what if the sheriff was involved?

He quickly took in the room, noting the door they'd entered through, and another, which was more than likely a closet. No escape route. If things became desperate, he could always go through the window, but that was a last resort.

"You can quit trying to find a way out," Nelson commented dryly. "There's no escape. You should've turned the children over to my boys, and we could've avoided all the dramatics."

Time. Time was best solution was for them to get out alive and for backup to arrive. Riggs straightened. "It's too late, Craddick. The FBI has already been notified."

Annie's gaze met his before going back to the man in charge.

Craddick smiled and waved his hand like he was swatting a fly. "You bore me. You're in over your head, Brenner. The kids will be gone in five minutes."

A pounding of feet sounded down the hallway and grew louder. At first Riggs was afraid the children were being brought to the van, but these heavy steps sounded like boots.

The two men who'd brought Riggs and Annie into

the home suddenly moved behind the desk, one on each side of Craddick. The door burst inward.

An armed man with gauge earrings broke through the door with a gun jabbed in Josie's back. Jonah was in Josie's arms, and Kay-Kay was at her side.

Fear gripped Riggs as he stared at the children.

Jonah clung to Josie's shirt. Kay-Kay's bottom lip trembled when she saw Craddick. The little girl buried her head in Josie's side and cried, "I want to go home."

No. No. No. This couldn't be happening. Jonah and Kay-Kay could not be taken again. Annie and he hadn't gone through all the danger only to lose the kids now.

He'd die first.

SEVENTEEN

Annie couldn't breathe. Petrified of witnessing her father take Jonah and Kay-Kay, she had to make her move. Recognition had not shown in his eyes.

How could a father forget his own child?

Her knees shook as she tried to get control of herself. But the children needed to be removed from the room now. *Please, God, save the children.*

A look of bored satisfaction crossed her father's face, and he waved his hand. "Get those kids out of here and take them to the caregivers."

Jonah and Kay-Kay screamed while clinging to Josie. Jonah glimpsed Riggs, and he almost leaped from Josie's arms. The baby held out his arms to Riggs and pumped his hands, crying.

"No!" Kay-Kay fought, but the man with the spinner chrome wheel earrings yanked her, breaking Kay-Kay's grip. The little girl's gaze landed on Annie, pleading with her to save her. "Tormy! Help me!"

Annie's breath hitched, a sharp pain in her heart. She refrained from grabbing for the children, knowing it would be safer for them not to be in the room. Letting them go was the hardest thing she'd ever endured. Holding back tears, she said, "It will be okay."

As soon as the men ushered the kids from the room, the sound of the cries faded.

Her father looked at the two remaining men. "Take these three out back, kill them and bury their bodies."

Annie's mouth dropped open at the callousness of her father's words. His attention went back to his laptop, like he had work to do. He could kill without a second thought. She took a step forward.

It was time for reckoning.

When his black eyes looked up at her, she drew a deep breath and announced coolly, "Nelson Craddick, I'm your daughter." She paused a split second to let her words sink in. "I'm going to take you down."

An incredulous look swallowed her father's face. "Annie?"

The gunman who'd taken the children returned to the room and stepped behind her. The other two men moved behind Josie and Riggs.

After years of sacrifice, training and planning, it all boiled down to this moment.

There was no room for mistakes.

Annie stepped to the right, putting her out of aim of the earring guy's gun, and grabbed the barrel. In one smooth motion, she jerked the barrel across her body and down like she was hoeing a garden.

Movement exploded as Riggs and Josie both fought with their assailants.

Annie's man tried to hang on and fell into her, the weight making her lose her balance. She fell to her side on the floor, but she didn't relinquish her grip. She shoved her shoulder into his kneecap. A loud *pop*. The man fell to the floor in agony.

Pain on her arm where the cougar had attacked shot through her, but she was barely aware. The need for survival outweighed all physical discomfort.

She got back to her feet with the weapon in her hand. Riggs had disarmed his man, and Josie still struggled with hers. Annie had taught the team members, including Josie, self-defense. Riggs went to assist Annie's partner, but was too late. The assailant aimed his gun at Annie. "Drop your weapon."

"No," her father yelled. He came up with a Glock and held his other hand in the air. "Don't shoot my daughter."

A shotgun barrel rammed through the door. Annie couldn't react as her own weapon was pointed at the man who held Josie.

"Don't do it, Nelson." The weak, feminine voice from behind the door shook. "Surrender."

Confusion hit Annie. Whose voice was that?

Her father raised his weapon.

Gunfire exploded in the room.

Annie ducked behind the desk but kept a tight grip on her gun. Her heart pounded. Where was Riggs? *Please, let Riggs be all right.*

As quickly as it started, silence filled the room except for the sickening sound of a groan.

She glanced around the desk to see Riggs kneeling with his gun ready and checking for a pulse on the gunman at his feet. Josie stood beside Riggs.

Suddenly, a loud commotion came from down the hall. Sheriff's deputies and members of Bliss's team stormed into the room.

Chandler Murphy, a team member, checked on Josie while another strode over to Annie.

"Are you all right?"

"Yes. But we need to find the children."

Chandler shook his head. "We caught them before the van left the driveway. The sheriff's deputies are arresting the men now while Bliss and Kennedy help with the children."

The breath whooshed from Annie with relief. Kennedy was the psychologist for the team and, besides providing therapy, helped with things like reunification of parents with their children. "Thank you." Annie's knees continued to shake—she still didn't believe it was over. As she headed toward her father, who lay on the floor behind his desk, Riggs came over and put an arm around her shoulder. She never would've made it through without him.

Her father opened his eyes and attempted to sit. "Tami shot me. I can't believe the weakling shot me."

He must've been referring to the woman who held the shotgun behind the door—the one who looked familiar. Annie knelt beside him. "Stay still. Paramedics will be here shortly." Her mouth felt like it was full of cotton, making her voice come out hoarse.

"My own daughter took me down. I've been keeping my eye on you, Annie. You…you rescue children." He blinked, and his breathing came in shallow gasps. A gaping wound below his collarbone bled. It was difficult to tell how close the bullet had come to his heart. Her dad's face turned whiter by the second, with almost a grayish tint.

Annie didn't respond. What could she say? She'd

dreamed of this moment for her whole life, but now only sadness filled her—for what could've been. "Rest."

He merely nodded and closed his eyes. "Jacobs."

She leaned over him. "What?"

Her father remained still and didn't respond.

She touched his wrist and felt a slight pulse. When she glanced at Riggs, his eyes overflowed with empathy.

"Nelson Craddick is my father."

He whispered, "I know."

"Make room," a deputy said. "Paramedics coming through."

Except for the wounded, everyone cleared out of the room. As Riggs left, he turned and mouthed, "I'll be out here."

She nodded and then moved back to give the man and woman paramedic duo room as they put her father on the stretcher. The scene was surreal. Purposely, she avoided looking at two of the gunmen with severe injuries as she moved for the open door. Standing in the corner with her head down, she waited while emergency responders loaded the three and moved from the room.

Quiet voices echoed through the hall and into the other rooms.

As soon as she stepped out, Riggs's arm went around her. They walked silently through the house and out of the back door. Under the shade of a mimosa tree, Riggs pulled her into a hug.

Tears ran down her cheeks to his shirt. He didn't say a word, as if sensing she needed this moment. And he was enough. His powerful arms held her, and his chin rested on the top of her head.

A clattering sounded as the medics loaded the injured into the waiting ambulances. As they wheeled her father by, they paused when she reached out and brushed a hand across his shoulder. His eyes remained closed, and his coloring was even paler than earlier.

Everyone silently looked on as the vehicles left the yard with their lights swirling.

"Tormy! Riggs!" Kay-Kay's voice had them turning.

"These children are eager to see you." Bliss Walker carried Jonah, and Kay-Kay stood at her side.

Annie smiled and wrapped her arms around them, squeezing gently and savoring the knowledge they were safe and going home. *Thank You, God, for saving them.*

"Pardner." Riggs gave Jonah a peck on the head and rested his hand on the girl's shoulder. He looked like he wanted to say something, but he stood there smiling with a glisten in his eyes instead.

"Are me and my brudder going home now?"

"Yeah, Kay-Kay bug, you're going home."

The girl's lip puckered. "I couldn't help Shotgun."

Annie and Riggs exchanged looks.

Riggs asked, "Where's Shotgun?"

"Josie put him away."

Concern ate at Annie until Josie walked over and patted the girl on the head. "The dog is fine. You did an excellent job taking care of him."

Kay-Kay beamed at her.

Josie glanced at Riggs and whispered, "When a truck screeched to a stop in front of the house and two men jumped out, I knew we'd been found. I was afraid the gunman might harm your dog, so I put him in the utility room and me and the kids ran out the backdoor. But one of the men was waiting for us. No time to use my gun"

"I'm sorry. You did the right thing," he mumbled. "Thanks for taking care of Shotgun."

Annie barely kept the tears at bay. A few minutes later, she and Riggs went back into the home to give the deputies a statement—a process that seemed to take forever.

"Where is Sheriff Ludlam?" Riggs asked.

The deputy looked at him. "I can't answer that at the moment."

Chandler motioned them over.

"Do you know something?" Annie asked.

He leaned in and spoke quietly. "I overheard one of the deputies mention Sheriff Ludlam is obtaining a search warrant for a local judge A man by the name of Jacobs. Seems the helicopter downed on Riggs's ranch belonged to the judge's family, and the sheriff believes Jacobs set you up to be attacked. Money is the downfall of many a good man. Do you know him?"

Annie glanced at Riggs, saw the pain in his eyes, and then looked back to her team member. "I've never talked with the judge, but I saw him on an online meeting with Nelson Craddick the night I rescued the kids." She still had a difficult time calling Craddick her dad.

Chandler nodded. "Hopefully, the authorities will be able to take down everyone involved."

After Chandler walked away, Riggs lowered his head and his shoulders dropped. "I never would've guessed Chad was involved. But the evidence connects. I'm glad my dad wasn't around to see this. Our family always admired the man. I never should've called him this morning and tipped him off."

Annie laid her hand on his shoulder and felt the tenseness of his muscles. "You couldn't have known."

Another deputy walked up with a clipboard and

asked Riggs, "Do you have time to answer a couple more questions?"

"Sure."

Annie leaned against a wall and tried to stay out of the way. She still couldn't believe it was over. During the brief respite, she noticed the lady with long scraggly hair—the woman who Annie thought looked familiar—also being questioned by a deputy. The deputy questioned her about the rifle and the shooting of Annie's father.

She's the one who shot my father.

When they were done, Annie stepped over. "I've seen you before, I think. I'm Annie Tillman."

"Tami Dillard." Her blue eyes squinted. "You look familiar, too, but there's been so many children through here for years I lose track. Were you housed here?"

"No." Shame once again filled Annie as she debated whether to tell the woman she was Craddick's daughter. Tami's brow furrowed, and then it hit Annie. "You were kidnapped from a homeless shelter thirteen years ago in Liberty, Texas."

Her mouth dropped open. "How did you know?"

Annie drew a deep breath. "I was in that van. Nelson Craddick is my father."

Tami pointed at her. "You were that girl? I remember. You sat in the back seat and offered me some of your SweeTarts."

"Yes." A smile formed. "I'd forgotten about that. What about your sister?"

The woman looked down. "I don't know. They sold Casey, I think. I was kept at this home to help tend to the younger children." She pointed to a mole on her cheek. "I was more valuable tending to the kids, but Casey was moved after two weeks."

Pain filled Annie, and she gently placed her hand on the woman's arm. "I will help you find your sister."

Tami's eyes grew large. "Do you think she's still alive?"

At first doubt crossed Annie's thoughts, but then she nodded. "Yes. I do. If God helped me find you, then He'll help us find Casey. I promise, I will not stop looking for your sister."

The woman's feeble smile warmed Annie's heart.

"I don't know what I'm going to do." Tami chewed on her bottom lip. "I've been here since I was a teen. I have no money. No training. I love children, but I don't know if I can support myself babysitting kids. As much as I hate what Craddick and Jacobs have done to children and their families, it's given me security."

Annie put a hand on her bony shoulder. "Bring the Children Home Project will help you. We have a psychologist who offers counseling, and I know of a few good shelters you can stay at until you get on your feet."

Tami shook her head. "I don't like shelters."

Oh, what had she been thinking? Tami had been stolen from a shelter. "We will help you find housing."

That seemed to appease her.

After most people had left, Annie turned to see Riggs waiting for her beside his truck, and she walked over to him.

He asked, "What's the plan?"

"The children are being brought back to the rental house while authorities contact parents. Jonah and Kay-Kay's parents will be easy, but others will have to be tracked down. Especially for the little ones who are not vocal."

He frowned. "It's a mess, isn't it?"

"Yes, it is." She looked at him. "Earlier, you said you knew I was Nelson Craddick's daughter. How did you know?"

He sighed. "In the FBI, I remembered looking at your father's file. In it was a family photo of your dad, mom and you. I knew you looked familiar, but I couldn't place you. If I'd known your last name was Craddick, it probably would've come to me."

She nodded. "It would've changed everything if you had recognized me and told me who I was earlier."

His gentle smile comforted her. He wrapped his arms around her waist and pulled her close, the warmth of his breath brushing her cheek. "Maybe this was the way it was supposed to be. We don't always understand God's plan. The kids were rescued, and the kidnapping ring will be brought to justice."

Riggs was right. Maybe she shouldn't question the how or why but take solace that children were safe, and her father wouldn't be free to hurt anyone again. That had been her dream for years.

The next day, late morning, Riggs stood outside a local police station and waited with Annie. Nelson Craddick had passed away during the night. Judge Chadwick Jacobs had lawyered up, but already several of the gunmen, including Waylon and Sonny, were naming him as the ringleader. Sadness for what the judge's family were going through hit Riggs hard, but the man needed to pay for his crimes. No doubt, Jacobs would put up a fight, but Riggs had confidence the mounting evidence would land the man in prison for many years.

A small SUV pulled into the parking lot. The vehicle had barely stopped before the passenger door swung open and a woman in her late twenties got out and raced across the pavement.

Kay-Kay yelled, "Mama."

She threw her arms into the air, and the woman—in between uncontrolled crying—grasped the girl in a tight hug. "I'm so glad to see you. I love you. I love you." The woman's mumblings sent a chill down Riggs's spine.

When Jonah heard the voice, he leaped with his hands outstretched, almost causing Bliss Walker to lose her grip. Mrs. Ferrell half laughed and cried as she took Jonah.

A man stood back with his hands in his pockets and rocked nervously on his heels.

"Daddy!" Kay-Kay ran to him.

It was then a lump formed in Riggs's throat that was impossible to swallow. His heart swelled at the reunion, and he couldn't help but think what he wouldn't do to have a meeting with Macy Sue just one more time. One more time to hear "Daddy" in her sweet voice.

Annie wrapped her arm in his and gave him a squeeze. "Remember this. When things get tough or don't turn out like we want, this memory will get you through."

Bliss Walker had stepped back to give the family room, a satisfied expression on her face.

After many tears and smiles, the parents profusely thanked Annie and Riggs for their help in finding the children.

Kay-Kay wrapped her arms around Annie. "Thank you." Then the girl turned her sights on him. "I love you."

"Aw. I love you, too, Kay-Kay bug." His throat tightened making his voice husky and difficult to keep it from cracking. He gave Jonah a peck on the head. "You, too, pardner."

After the parents left with the kids, Bliss and Josie walked over to where Riggs and Annie were standing. Bliss said, "Mr. Brenner, we appreciate your help in finding and rescuing the children. If you ever want a job with our team, just call me."

He took the business card the owner of the program held out. "Thanks. I'll consider the offer."

"See that you do." The woman turned back to Annie. "And next week, I want you to make an appointment to visit with Kennedy."

"I'm not sure that's going to be necessary." Annie's gaze connected with the serious blue eyes of her boss. Even before Bliss responded, Annie held up her hands. "Never mind. After suffering with amnesia and bringing down my father, I can see I don't have a leg to stand on. Besides, Kennedy is the best."

Bliss merely nodded and walked away.

Riggs glanced at Annie. He didn't ask questions about the appointment her boss had ordered for he figured it'd be difficult for her to seek help much like it had been for him after Claire's and Macy Sue's death. Instead, he took her hand, and they strolled to his vehicle.

"I've never seen my boss offer someone a job like that." Annie smiled and shrugged. "Well, except for me."

"So, I'm in a special category now?" He chuckled.

"Certainly. Up there with the best. You should seriously consider that offer."

He grew serious as his hands squeezed hers. "I don't want our relationship to end, Annie. I'm ready to live again, and I'd like you to be a part of it. My life has been empty, and I'm ready to risk my heart to have you in it." Her green eyes flashed with emotion he couldn't read, but he didn't care what her reaction was. He had to take the chance that she'd agree to keep seeing him. Those beautiful lips captivated him, and he bent down and pressed his mouth to hers. She melted in his arms. "I've fallen in love with you, Annie."

A smile crossed her shiny lips. "Even though you know who I am? The daughter of a criminal—the type of man we fight every day."

"I know who your father is, but you have nothing but good in your heart. Don't you see that?"

She wrapped her arms around his neck. "You make me the happiest person in the world, Riggs Brenner. I love you, too."

EPILOGUE

Eighteen months later

Annie crouched in an offensive position, her hands out front, ready to make her move.

Riggs's gaze connected with hers as they circled one another, both leery. "Don't take your attention off the target," he taunted.

Shotgun barked.

"Stay, boy. I got this."

She didn't respond as sweat dripped down her face and she readied herself for a sweeping foot—Riggs's most favored move. She watched, keeping her attention on his body, not his facial expression that was attempting to distract her. His hand came up quickly, and she deflected it with her right as she took a step to the left and karate chopped him in the neck. She wrapped her arm around his neck and used her hip to throw him to the mat.

He landed with a groan.

Silence, followed by a burst of cheers and claps.

A smile crossed her lips.

Shotgun ran to Riggs and licked his face. Riggs laughed and said, "Okay, boy. I'm all right."

Whitney, a lanky fourteen-year-old student, beamed at Annie. "Oh, please, Mrs. Brenner, show me how to do that."

Riggs climbed to his feet. "My wife can't wait to show you how to perform her moves."

Even though they'd been married just over a year, hearing Riggs call her his wife was still surreal.

He glanced at Annie and shook his head. After the girls had moved back against the wall, he whispered, "You were ready for that one."

"You give yourself away, hubby dear. I've told you that. You turn your foot in preparation. It's your telltale."

Riggs's eyes shined, and his face turned serious. "You're feeling all right, though?"

She sighed and smiled. "I'll get Josie to fill in for me for the next several months, until after the baby comes."

He gave her a peck on the cheek. "I'd appreciate that."

Forty-five minutes later, after the class was over, they grabbed something to eat and headed to the canyon. As they pulled up to their new cabin—complete with a wraparound porch, a colorful array of flowers in a wooden barrel and rocking chairs facing the west—a sense of home and belonging filled her.

Riggs let Shotgun out of the back of the cab, and the canine leaped to the ground.

Without having to say a word, Annie and Riggs headed for the back porch. She removed her cell phone and had it ready in her hand.

"Do you have plenty of signal?"

She laughed. "Are you kidding me? With the mega amplifier that you bought for the house?"

"Just checking. You can never be too sure."

Colossal thunderheads built to the west, and rays of the setting sun burst behind the clouds, promising a spectacular storm to come.

Annie ignored the rockers but went straight for the oversize porch swing. "It's beautiful, isn't it?"

Riggs settled beside her, took her hand and pressed his lips to her fingers. "Yes, you are."

She shook her head, but a grin spread across her lips.

He put his arm around her, and she snuggled into his embrace. Lightning streaked across the sky in the distance. "It's going to be a good one. Maybe as electric as the one when we first met."

"Hard to believe it's been a year and a half since I woke up on that ledge. My life has changed so much for the better since that day. Who knew how good life could be? And I'm so glad you joined the Bring the Children Home Project."

"I wished there weren't a need, but until every child is found and brought home, I can't see ever giving it up. Especially with us about to have one of our own."

"Me, either." Annie used to fret what kind of mom she'd be, but she didn't worry anymore. She had faith in her God and in her husband.

"I love you, Annie Brenner."

"Right back at you, Riggs Brenner."

Her phone lit up like clockwork, the first Saturday of every month, and both jumped to answer on the first ring. Kay-Kay and Jonah's smiling images stared back at them.

"Kay-Kay bug and pardner!" Riggs's voice held laughter.

Life just kept getting better and better.

* * * * *

If you liked this story from Connie Queen,
check out her previous
Love Inspired Suspense books:

Justice Undercover
Texas Christmas Revenge

Available now from Love Inspired Suspense!

Find more great reads at www.LoveInspired.com.

Dear Reader,

When I was a child, my family used to travel every year to watch the outdoor musical in Palo Duro Canyon. I've always wanted to set a story there, and I'm happy you've joined me in my journey to the rugged and beautiful land of West Texas.

Have you ever been overwhelmed with problems? Hopefully, you've never had amnesia or had gunmen chasing you through a canyon, but I think we've all struggled with obstacles stacked in front of us. Both Annie and Riggs had a tough past, but they build on their faith and stay true to what they believe in.

How did you tackle issues? Do you trust in God or try to handle it yourself?

I love to hear from readers! You can connect with me at www.conniequeenauthor.com or on my Facebook page at www.facebook.com/queenofheartthrobbing-suspense.

Connie Queen

COMING NEXT MONTH FROM
Love Inspired Suspense

READY TO PROTECT
Rocky Mountain K-9 Unit • by Valerie Hansen

After witnessing a congresswoman's murder, wildlife photographer and mother-to-be Jamie London is forced into the protection of K-9 cop Ben Sawyer and police dog Shadow. But when they're tracked down by the assassin, are Ben and Shadow enough to guarantee Jamie will make it to the hearing alive?

FUGITIVE HUNT
Justice Seekers • by Laura Scott

Surviving an attack by her serial murderer cousin years ago left police officer Morganne Kimball his number one target. Now that he's escaped prison, her only choice is to team up with US deputy marshal Colt Nelson to capture him before she becomes his next victim...

DEATH VALLEY HIDEOUT
Desert Justice • by Dana Mentink

Placed in the WITSEC program while his brother testifies against a terrifying criminal, Tony Ortega must guard his young niece and nephew—especially with a hit man hunting for them. Death Valley local Willow Duke's hideout might just be the difference between the little family's life or death...

UNSOLVED ABDUCTION
by Jill Elizabeth Nelson

Widowed Carina Collins can't remember her parents' murder or her own kidnapping. But when she and her eighteen-month-old son are attacked in their new home, neighbor Ryder Jameson is convinced the two incidents are related. Can she put the pieces of the past together in time to live to see a future?

TEXAS KILLER CONNECTION
Cowboy Lawmen • by Virginia Vaughan

Former army intelligence officer Brooke Moore is determined to solve the murder of her look-alike cousin, Tessa—and now she's become the killer's next target. Blaming himself for his ex Tessa's death, FBI agent Colby Avery welcomes the new leads Brooke turns up. But digging deeper brings danger straight to their doorstep...

PERILOUS WILDERNESS ESCAPE
by Rhonda Starnes

Hot on the trail of a ruthless drug cartel, FBI agent Randy Ingalls is nearly killed in an ambush—and left with amnesia. Can Agent Katherine Lewis decipher the clues in his lost memory, or will she lose the case—and her partner—for good?

LISCNM0322

Get 4 FREE REWARDS!

We'll send you 2 FREE Books plus 2 FREE Mystery Gifts.

FREE Value Over **$20**

Both the **Love Inspired®** and **Love Inspired® Suspense** series feature compelling novels filled with inspirational romance, faith, forgiveness, and hope.

YES! Please send me 2 FREE novels from the Love Inspired or Love Inspired Suspense series and my 2 FREE gifts (gifts are worth about $10 retail). After receiving them, if I don't wish to receive any more books, I can return the shipping statement marked "cancel." If I don't cancel, I will receive 6 brand-new Love Inspired Larger-Print books or Love Inspired Suspense Larger-Print books every month and be billed just $5.99 each in the U.S. or $6.24 each in Canada. That is a savings of at least 17% off the cover price. It's quite a bargain! Shipping and handling is just 50¢ per book in the U.S. and $1.25 per book in Canada.* I understand that accepting the 2 free books and gifts places me under no obligation to buy anything. I can always return a shipment and cancel at any time. The free books and gifts are mine to keep no matter what I decide.

Choose one: ☐ **Love Inspired**
Larger-Print
(122/322 IDN GNWC)

☐ **Love Inspired Suspense**
Larger-Print
(107/307 IDN GNWN)

Name (please print)

Address   Apt. #

City   State/Province   Zip/Postal Code

Email: Please check this box ☐ if you would like to receive newsletters and promotional emails from Harlequin Enterprises ULC and its affiliates. You can unsubscribe anytime.

Mail to the **Harlequin Reader Service:**
IN U.S.A.: P.O. Box 1341, Buffalo, NY 14240-8531
IN CANADA: P.O. Box 603, Fort Erie, Ontario L2A 5X3

Want to try 2 free books from another series? Call 1-800-873-8635 or visit www.ReaderService.com.

*Terms and prices subject to change without notice. Prices do not include sales taxes, which will be charged (if applicable) based on your state or country of residence. Canadian residents will be charged applicable taxes. Offer not valid in Quebec. This offer is limited to one order per household. Books received may not be as shown. Not valid for current subscribers to the Love Inspired or Love Inspired Suspense series. All orders subject to approval. Credit or debit balances in a customer's account(s) may be offset by any other outstanding balance owed by or to the customer. Please allow 4 to 6 weeks for delivery. Offer available while quantities last.

Your Privacy—Your information is being collected by Harlequin Enterprises ULC, operating as Harlequin Reader Service. For a complete summary of the information we collect, how we use this information and to whom it is disclosed, please visit our privacy notice located at corporate.harlequin.com/privacy-notice. From time to time we may also exchange your personal information with reputable third parties. If you wish to opt out of this sharing of your personal information, please visit readerservice.com/consumerschoice or call 1-800-873-8635. **Notice to California Residents**—Under California law, you have specific rights to control and access your data. For more information on these rights and how to exercise them, visit corporate.harlequin.com/california-privacy.

LIRLIS22